"You agreed to the terms of our marriage."

Brant's voice was dry, his mouth twisted in a lopsided smile.

"I know I did, but it's one thing to agree to be your wife on paper and quite another to accept the reality of our marriage."

"So you got cold feet," he murmured contemplatively. "Where's the woman who was begging me to make love to her a few weeks ago? Of course I'd just given you a diamond-and-emerald necklace. Was that where I went wrong last night?"

Without thinking, her hand swung out in a stinging blow to his face. As soon as she had done it, she was horrified. "Oh, Brant, I'm sorry. I didn't mean to do that . . . you just went too far."

"On the contrary, I don't think I've gone far enough, that's the whole problem."

Kathryn Ross was born in Zambia, where her parents happened to live at that time, but was educated in Ireland and England, where she now lives in a village near Blackpool in Lancashire. She enjoys her work as a professional beauty therapist, but the main love of her life is writing. Kathryn doesn't remember a time when she wasn't scribbling—her first novel at the age of ten was a children's adventure story, unpublished but terrific! Traveling and the friends made through it have been a real pleasure. Candlelit dinners, log fires on a winter's night and long walks in the Lake District are also special joys. She says she's naturally romantic, enjoying reading as well as writing romance fiction. Still single—Mr. Right hasn't come along yet—Kathryn admits her boyfriends have tough competition from her fictional heroes.

PLAYING BY THE RULES
Kathryn Ross

Harlequin Books

TORONTO • NEW YORK • LONDON
AMSTERDAM • PARIS • SYDNEY • HAMBURG
STOCKHOLM • ATHENS • TOKYO • MILAN
MADRID • WARSAW • BUDAPEST • AUCKLAND

Original hardcover edition published in 1991
by Mills & Boon Limited

ISBN 0-373-17109-9

Harlequin Romance first edition May 1992

PLAYING BY THE RULES

CHAPTER ONE

THE law firm of Harcourt McConell was situated in the centre of Toronto. A large impressive building that towered into the air, its many glass windows reflected the early morning sunlight.

Kelsey McConell drove her silver BMW down into the underground car park and into her reserved space, but instead of grabbing her briefcase and rushing towards the elevator as she usually did on a Monday morning she took time to check her appearance in the mirror on her sun visor.

As always, her long honey-gold hair was sitting perfectly, its sleek well-groomed style framing the attractive heart-shaped face. Today, however, she wore more make-up than normal, and although she had applied it skilfully it did little to hide the fact that she had cried too many tears just recently.

Taking a deep steadying breath, she picked up her briefcase and stepped out of the car. It had been a bad idea to take time off work last week; it hadn't helped. She was best keeping busy—when her mind was fully occupied she wouldn't have time to dwell on things.

Her secretary, Maggie Thornton, had just stepped into the lift ahead of her, and she held the doors for her boss, a look of surprise on her young face. 'Kelsey, we didn't expect you back until next week! Mr Harcourt said——'

'Yes, I know what Brant Harcourt has said.' She cut across the girl impatiently and stabbed one well-manicured nail at floor twenty on the wall panel. 'But I couldn't stay away any longer, especially now with all the extra work that must have accumulated on my desk.'

There was a silence for a moment, a rather uncomfortable one, Kelsey thought, and she flicked a glance over at the other girl in puzzlement.

'We are all very sorry about your grandfather,' Maggie said softly.

'Yes.' Kelsey relaxed back against the wall. People were always strained and hesitant when it came to talking about death, and nobody knew what to say to make it better, Kelsey least of all. 'I'm going to miss him,' she answered simply.

Her eyes moved to the gold name-plates above the rows of buttons, proclaiming that they were in the domain of Harcourt and McConell, attorneys of law, and the same thought flitted through her mind as it always did when she glanced at it. Her grandfather's name should come first—he was the one who had established the business, who had earned it its prestigious reputation, and that was long before Brant Harcourt had arrived on the scene. The doors swished open on the twentieth floor and both girls stepped out. A long corridor led down through rows of glass-fronted, soundproof offices; each one was occupied with people preparing for the busy day ahead. Most of them noticed Kelsey as she walked past, and she could almost hear the whispers of speculation that followed her progress down towards her office.

Before she could open her door the one beside it shot open, and Daniel Marsden came out. As usual he was stylishly dressed: a grey suit sat precisely on his broad-shouldered frame; a blue silk tie exactly matched the colour of his eyes. Kelsey always thought that he looked like a model from an expensive clothing store.

'Kelsey, we didn't expect you back so soon! Brant said he'd given orders that you were to have two weeks' leave.'

A glimmer of annoyance lit her green eyes for a moment, and she had to bite down a sarcastic reply.

Only Brant Harcourt could make an offer to take a vacation sound like an ultimatum.

'I didn't want any more time off,' she answered calmly. 'I'd rather be back at work.' She would have followed her secretary into her office then, except that Daniel was not about to let her escape before he got to the real point of interest.

'What's happening about your grandfather's holdings, Kelsey? His real estate buisness and all the land he owns, will it revert to you?'

'My grandfather's will has not been read yet.' Her reply was deliberately non-committal. 'And I honestly don't know what will be in it.'

Daniel nodded. 'I think it's a foregone conclusion, though. Everyone in the building is expecting you to inherit. There's no one else for him to leave everything to, is there?'

'No other relatives, no,' Kelsey answered carefully.

Daniel's face lit up with a rakish grin. 'You are going to be one powerful lady, Kel; I knew I was on to a good thing the day I started to date you. Don't forget that you promised to have dinner with me next week, and then there is George's retirement party at the weekend.'

'How could I possibly forget when you keep ringing me up to remind me?' she answered light-heartedly.

Daniel laughed at that. 'Well, I do believe in keeping a couple of steps ahead of the competition, and I imagine it's going to get very stiff when you inherit the McConell real estate business. You're going to be in charge of quite an empire.'

'You are incorrigible, Daniel Marsden,' Kelsey said with a shake of her head—but she had to laugh.

She felt a little more cheerful as she opened the door into her office. Daniel's good humour was infectious, and his certainty that the McConell holdings would indeed go to her made her feel a little more confident than she had done previously.

'Get Brant on the phone and tell him I'm in, will you,

Maggie?' she asked her secretary on the way past. Not that he wouldn't know already, she thought with a sigh, as she closed the connecting door between them. Brant would have known of her arrival the moment she set foot in the building. She didn't sit down at her desk immediately, but stood at the large picture windows looking out over the Toronto skyline.

Was Daniel right? Would she inherit the McConell business holdings? Niggling doubts threatened to surface again and she tried to fight them down. Of course she would inherit her grandfather's estate; she was his only living relative—they were her birthright.

She turned away from the view and ran a distracted hand through silky hair. She had been pursuing a stake in the family businesses for quite some time now, but she had never wanted to get it in this way. In fact it was only last year that she had asked her grandfather if she could buy some shares in the McConell real estate business, which was linked very closely to the law firm. The answer had been an unequivocal no. She had been bitterly disappointed and very hurt, especially when she found out that he had sold a substantial amount of shares in McConell Real Estate to Brant Harcourt soon after, when Brant had entered the law firm as his partner. That man seemed to have fingers in every profitable firm in town. He also had a habit of getting under Kelsey's skin.

Brant Harcourt was a brilliant lawyer. When he had come into partnership with her grandfather a year ago, he had brought more business than they could cope with. To enable them to handle it they had decided to take on two junior partners. Kelsey had jumped at the chance. She was a well-qualified lawyer, experienced, had worked within the firm for a few years; ideal for the position—or so she had thought. Brant, however, had had different ideas on that subject, and the place that she had wanted had been offered to Daniel Marsden, who had far less experience than Kelsey, plus the fact that he was twenty-six and nearly two years younger than she was. Kelsey had accepted the decision with good grace, but deep down it had rankled, and she had never quite forgiven Brant Harcourt.

At that moment the door opened, and the subject of her thoughts strode in. As always, the very sight of him seemed to alert every nerve-ending within her; it was like a silent alarm system warning her against relaxing her guard for one second in his presence. As she met his dark steady gaze all her natural defences were firmly up.

'I thought I told you to have at least another week off,' the velvet voice demanded, without preamble.

She shrugged, and folded her arms across her slender figure in a gesture that was more protective than relaxed. 'You did, but I didn't realise that it was an order,' she answered quietly. 'Should I have come upstairs and asked permission to sit at my desk?'

He wasn't amused by her flippancy. The dark eyes lingered on her pale skin and the dark shadows beneath gold-green eyes with equanimity. 'I suppose you know that your grandfather's will is being read tomorrow?'

She inclined her head coolly and studied him surreptitiously from beneath long dark lashes. A dark tailor-made suit emphasised powerful shoulders and a lithe, superbly fit body. Hair as black as a raven's wing sat neatly in place, a few strands of silver only daring to appear at his temples. The overall effect was as suavely stylish as Daniel Marsden's look, but there was one main difference. Daniel's appearance was carefully contrived to give the illusion of sex appeal, whereas Brant Harcourt possessed the real thing without having to work at it. That raw sexuality, combined with a cool, pragmatic manner, could fire your blood and then intimidate you at one and the same time.

'Have you any idea what it will contain?'

That question made her lift her eyes to his with feigned confidence. 'I would say it's pretty safe to assume that my grandfather has left all of his shares in McConell Real Estate to me, plus the rest of his holdings, wouldn't

you?' In her effort to conceal her uncertainty about this
her tone was just a little too smug.

He didn't reveal by one flicker of an eyelash any
opinion that he had on the subject. 'As Joe McConell
was fond of saying, "there is nothing sure in this world
except death and taxes".'

Kelsey gave a small smile. 'Well, let's say that I am
quietly confident.' She leaned back against the window-
sill, looking poised and elegant in the pale powder-blue
suit. 'Considering you own a few shares in McConell
Real Estate, I suppose this will mean we will be almost
like partners.' She slanted a bold look up at him. 'How
do you feel about that?' Even as she spoke she marvelled
at her own temerity. It was an unequivocal fact that
Brant would resent her involvement in that business at
top level. He hadn't thought her good enough to be a
junior partner here, let alone a controlling partner of a
business he had invested heavily in.

She had to admire the way he kept his expression so
cool and impassive. This man gave nothing away—it
was probably one of the reasons why he was such a
formidable opponent in a court of law.

'Strange that you should ask that question.' The firm
mouth tugged into a lop-sided smile, giving Kelsey the
uneasy feeling that he was laughing at her. 'I was about
to ask you out to dinner this evening so that we could
discuss that very subject.'

Her eyes widened at this. Obviously, Brant wasn't as
unconcerned about matters as he liked to appear. They
had lunched together on a few occasions when business
had demanded it, and there had been a few dinner
parties when they had found themselves seated together
by chance, usually with their respective dates on either
side; but he had never actually asked her out to dinner
before. What was the idea? she wondered grimly. Was
he going to turn on his dazzling charm in the hope that
she would be so bemused and enchanted by him that she
would be an easy touch to manipulate when she had

control of McConell Real Estate? If he thought that, then he had miscalculated for once in his life. She was nobody's fool. Maybe he was going to offer to buy her out? Now, that was infinitely more feasible. No matter what he offered she wasn't about to sell, but curiosity prompted her to accept his invitation, anyway.

Before she could say anything, however, he was arrogantly taking her acceptance for granted.

'I'll pick you up about eight.'

As far as he was concerned the conversation was closed, and he walked towards the door with a lazy stride that set Kelsey's teeth on edge. She hated to be taken for granted by anyone—least of all him.

'Actually, I have a date tonight with Daniel,' she found herself telling him quickly. 'Perhaps we could make it another time?'

He turned with his hand on the door-handle. 'Cancel your date,' he instructed drily. 'What we have to talk about is more important.'

'To *you*, maybe.' Her anger flared at his imperious attitude. For all he knew her supposed date could be very important to her. 'Anyway, don't you think that you are being a bit premature? McConell Real Estate is not mine yet, and a few moments ago you were warning me about the perils of being complacent.' She gave him a cool smile. 'We'll talk when the company is officially mine.'

One dark eyebrow rose in an impassive face. 'My dear Kelsey, maybe I haven't made myself clear.' His voice was low, and somehow menacing. 'I know exactly what the terms of your grandfather's will are, and I can assure you that it is in your best interests to be well prepared for its reading.'

The calm self-assured smile faded from her face at those words, and she could only look at him with wide startled eyes.

'Eight o'clock,' he reminded her abruptly, and, turning, he left the room.

Kelsey watched him through the glass partition as he stopped to say something to Maggie. It took all her powers of self-control not to rush out after him and demand to know what knowledge he had of Joe McConell's last will and testament. How had he gained access to confidential information? Maybe he hadn't; maybe he was just bluffing. After all, the man was a master of subterfuge in a court of law. His cases were conducted with a brilliant strategy; like a chess player his moves were subtle, concealing the fact that he was progressing in for the kill.

He left the outer office, and as he closed the door their eyes met and held for just a second through the glass. The impact of that dark gaze sent a tremor of apprehension racing down her spine.

Try as she might, Kelsey could not shake those feelings of disquiet all day. In fact, as the afternoon wore on they grew worse, and it became more difficult to concentrate on the tedious intricacy of corporate law. At five o'clock she closed the files that she had been working on with a snap, and flicked the intercom beside her. 'Maggie, could you find out if Brant is in his office, please?'

The answer came back a few minutes later. 'Yes, he is, Kelsey, and he is free if you want to go up.'

'Thanks,' Kelsey said drily. She didn't want to go up at all, but then she didn't want to wait until this evening to hear what he had to say. Taking a deep breath, she forced herself to go up and get it over with.

As the lift slid open on the top floor, however, she felt as if her courage had deserted her somewhere en route. Perhaps she was playing this all wrong and she should wait until this evening to hear what he had to say. Coming up here was tantamount to admitting how insecure she felt over her grandfather's will, and vulnerable was the last thing that she wanted to appear in front of Brant Harcourt. Her steps faltered before they reached his office door, and quite suddenly she changed direction and opened the door opposite, instead.

Her grandfather's domain was just as it had always been. The large office was impressive, to say the least. Thick blue carpets, dark oak-panelled walls, some completely lined with heavy reference volumes, and then, of course, there was the enormous desk where Joe McConell had spent most of his days. She crossed towards it, and then on impulse went to sit behind it. Her head rested back against the dark leather chair, and her eyes swept the room before lingering on the gold-framed photograph of her father that was given pride of place on the desk.

By rights, her grandfather's shares in McConell Real Estate should have gone to his son. He was the one who had run the business; his ideas had turned it into the thriving concern it was now; and it would have been Joe's greatest wish to leave it all to him. But destiny had decreed that that was not to be. Both of Kelsey's parents had been killed in a tragic car accident when she was just ten years of age. For a moment, the photograph became blurred through a haze of tears.

'What are you doing in here, Kelsey?' The softly spoken question made her jump, and she turned startled eyes towards the door to see Brant standing just inside, watching her.

'I thought I'd take this opportunity to clear away a few personal items from Joe's desk.' She hurriedly opened a drawer, glad of the excuse to hide her eyes from him.

'That's why you rang up and asked if you could see me, is it?' he enquired drily.

She didn't answer, but continued to root through the contents of the drawer, without really seeing anything. She couldn't hear him crossing the room, but she was conscious of the fact that he was doing so, and her hands trembled alarmingly as they went through the charade of being busy.

'Well, Kelsey?' He leaned against the desk, and, before she could avoid him his hand reached out to capture her chin and tip her head gently up towards him.

His dark gaze moved ruthlessly over her pale skin and the over-bright glitter of her emerald eyes. 'Just came up to do a bit of tidying, hmm?' The gentle, teasing tone just seemed to flay at her overwrought emotions, and she lifted a hand to knock his away with more force than was really necessary.

'I don't need to invent excuses for coming in here,' she told him, her eyes flashing with anger now. 'And I don't need to ask your permission to clear out my grandfather's personal files and effects; they are nothing to do with the law firm and they are nothing to do with you.'

'No?' One dark eyebrow rose. 'But then they don't belong to you, either.'

'Not until tomorrow, if we are going to be pedantically precise,' she shot back archly, and met his gaze with far more confidence than she was feeling. What was it her grandfather used to say? 'Be a lion in your face even if you are a deer in your heart'.

For a moment a gleam of amusement lit the rugged features. 'Oh, I see, you've come up here to read through the real estate files and acquaint yourself with being in charge of the business.' He straightened up. 'Well, all I can say is enjoy the fantasy while you can.'

'And what is that supposed to mean?' she demanded sharply.

He didn't answer, but the amusement faded from his eyes to be replaced by a serious look that made Kelsey's heartbeats increase with painful thuds.

She closed the drawer beside her with a resounding slam. 'Don't torment me, Brant,' she said softly now, all pretence at self-assurance deserting her suddenly. 'You know why I came up here. I need to know whatever it is that you are going to tell me now. I can't wait until this evening,' she admitted in a husky tone.

For a moment she thought that he still was not going to answer, then his lips twisted in a grim smile. 'What took you so long? I've been expecting you since I left your office this morning.'

'I've shown remarkable restraint, wouldn't you say?' she managed to answer lightly, and, getting stiffly to her feet, she crossed to the large picture windows behind her to stare out over the panoramic view of Toronto. It occurred to her that they were both prevaricating needlessly. Maybe Brant was as loath to tell her what he knew as she was to hear it?

'My grandfather has not left me his shares in McConell Real Estate, has he?' The question was a mere whisper in the silence of the room. In the few seconds that it took him to answer her she felt sure that he could hear the erratic beats of her heart, for they seemed to be filling her own ears with an intense and awful pounding.

'No.' The deep voice was unequivocal, and Kelsey closed her eyes, glad that she had her back towards him and that he couldn't see the expression on her face.

She allowed herself a few moments to compose her wayward emotions, and when she broke the silence her voice was amazingly calm and controlled. 'I suppose when it boils right down to it I'm not really surprised.' She turned around and there was a curiously poignant look on her young face. 'My grandfather never allowed me to have anything to do with that business. He didn't even like my working here.' She gave him a tremulous smile. 'He had some very old-fashioned ideas about women in the workplace; consequently, he never believed in making anything easy for me where my career was concerned.'

Brant's lips twisted in a sardonic smile. 'He did give you a job in one of the city's leading law establishments.'

A gleam of anger flared in her eyes. Brant was probably one of a large group of people who believed her career had been cushioned by the fact that she was Joe McConell's granddaughter; nothing could be further from the truth. She opened her mouth to put him straight on a few things, and then closed it again. Brant would probably not believe her if she told him the struggle she had had to be allowed to pursue her career; how she had had to be twice as good as the other applicants who had wanted a job here. She had worked herself into the ground to get a position here, but not only would Brant not believe that, he probably would not understand the reasons that had driven her relentlessly towards it.

He was watching her with a cool, derisive expression. He was probably gloating, she thought furiously. He thought that she was a spoilt little brat who had everything too easy; he had made that very clear a long time ago.

'Well, don't you want to know what Joe has decided to do with his shares in McConell Real Estate?' he asked in a silky tone that made her blood boil.

'They will be sold to the highest bidder, I presume,' she answered, with careless indifference. 'And I suppose I will get a nice little annuity out of it.'

He shook his head. 'Oh, no, Kelsey—it's not quite that straightforward.'

She frowned. 'What, then?'

The dark eyes glittered, but gave nothing away. 'With one proviso your grandfather has left all of his shares to me.' If his pause was for dramatic effect then he need not have bothered with it, for his next words were electrifying. 'The proviso being that in order to get them I have to marry you.'

CHAPTER TWO

'WELL, there you have it, Kelsey.' Harold Bremner tipped his glasses and stared at the pale young woman who sat opposite. 'If it's any consolation, your grandfather's will provides very adequately for you, even though its terms are somewhat unusual.'

It wasn't any consolation, but Kelsey forbore to comment. She had hardly said more than two words since she had entered the office, and she hadn't even glanced in Brant's direction. She supposed she should have been prepared for the fact that he would be here, but somehow she hadn't fully believed what Brant had told her yesterday. She couldn't comprehend how her grandfather could have done this to her.

The attorney returned his attention to the papers in front of him. 'You stand to inherit most of Joe's estate—except, of course, for the question of McConell Real Estate.'

'Which just happens to be worth more than everything else put together,' Kelsey murmured, in a dry voice. It also just happened to be the one thing she really wanted.

'Well, as I mentioned earlier, your grandfather has left you an option on the real estate shares,' Harold murmured.

Kelsey didn't think she had been left with any option at all, but she said nothing.

'As the situation stands. . .' Harold leafed through the documents in front of him until he found the relevant information '. . . Joe's fifty-one shares in McConell Real Estate——'

'Fifty-one per cent?' Kelsey interrupted him sharply, a puzzled frown marring her face. 'He owned eighty per cent, didn't he?'

'No.' Harold cleared his throat. 'Joe held fifty-one shares in the business; Mr Harcourt holds the remaining forty-nine per cent.'

For the first time, Kelsey looked directly at Brant. 'Joe gave you forty-nine shares of the family business!' Her tone was totally outraged, and her face burnt with angry colour.

'I can assure you that I paid a very healthy price for those shares, Kelsey. I was not given them,' Brant replied calmly, his dark eyes meeting her gaze steadily.

Kelsey shook her head. 'He never told me he was selling so many shares,' she murmured dazedly.

Harold cleared his throat again and broke the brief, heavy silence that had enveloped the office. 'Perhaps you would like me to read through the part of the will that deals with McConell Real Estate again?'

'I don't think that is necessary, Harold,' Brant told him drily. 'We've both got the picture. In the event of a marriage between Kelsey and myself, I will receive the remaining fifty-one shares in the business. How long have we got before we have to make a decision on this?' he asked in a brisk, businesslike tone that was like sandpaper over Kelsey's raw nerves.

The attorney returned his attention to the papers in front of him. 'About two months. If at the end of that time the two of you have not married, then the shares will be split into units and sold on the open market. There will be a stipulation attached to the sale that no more than ten units can be purchased by any one person. Kelsey will automatically receive ten shares.' Harold took off his glasses and looked across at the younger man. 'That ensures rather effectively that you remain the largest shareholder and at the head of the company, Mr Harcourt.'

'It also ensures effectively that I cannot buy full control of the company,' Brant stated in a harsh tone. 'And the only way I can get that is by marrying Kelsey.'

Kelsey's heart thudded painfully against her ribs and

her hands clenched into tight fists, but she said nothing, and her gaze never wavered from Harold's age-lined face.

'Er—yes, that is just about the sum of it,' he agreed, and polished his glasses with slow, meticulous care before pushing them firmly back on the bridge of his nose. 'In the event of your marriage you will have free reign in the day-to-day running of McConell Real Estate. Kelsey in return will receive a substantial cut of the profits at the end of each fiscal year. The proviso being, of course, that you are living as man and wife. Financially, you both have a lot to gain from marriage, but in the event of a divorce I'm afraid you would both lose a considerable——'

Kelsey's chair scraped back against the floor as she got hurriedly to her feet. She couldn't stand to hear any more of this. 'Thank you, Harold, but I've heard enough,' she stated firmly.

The lawyer looked up in surprise. 'But I haven't finished, there are several more pages on this.'

'I'm sure there are, but I think I've caught the bottom line.' She gave the worried-looking man a tight, strained smile, but didn't dare look at Brant as she turned and left the room.

She was shivering uncontrollably by the time she reached the door out on to the street, and it wasn't just from the cool autumn air. She lingered in the doorway for just a moment, watching the heavy rain bouncing off the pavements, then, pulling the collar of her trenchcoat up around her hair, she started to run out into it.

Before she had got very far, a strong hand took hold of her arm. 'Come on, my car is just around the corner.'

Brant didn't give her a chance to argue with him; before she could even draw breath he was bundling her into the front seat of his white Rolls-Royce.

'I don't need a lift,' she rounded on him furiously, as soon as he got behind the wheel.

'Did you bring your car?' he asked, with infuriating calm.

'No, I took a cab——'

'Then you need a lift.' The powerful engine purred into life and the car moved smoothly out into the flow of heavy traffic. She watched the strong, capable hands on the wheel; there was a glint of gold from a Gucci watch. It was nearly lunchtime, and Kelsey hadn't been into work yet. She just hadn't been able to face it this morning. Her mind had been numb with shock since leaving the offices yesterday, and it was only when she had walked into Harold Bremner's office and found Brant sitting back so arrogantly in an adjacent chair to her that things had started to sink in. The silence between them now stretched by uncomfortable degrees.

She turned her head away from him and stared out at the dull, miserable day. Her thoughts were so wild and chaotic that it was a while before she realised that he was not driving her back to the offices. 'Where are you taking me?' she demanded in a brittle tone that sounded as if it would snap at any moment.

'You make it sound as if I'm kidnapping you.' His dry humour did nothing to relieve the tension. 'I thought as we didn't make dinner last night that we could have lunch together.'

'I don't want to have lunch with you. In fact, I don't want to be in your company for one second longer than is absolutely necessary.' She bit the words out furiously and her whole body was shaking with the force of her emotion.

'Oh, for heaven's sake!' He pulled the car off the road, and put on the hand-brake with a violent jerking movement. 'Don't vent your anger at your grandfather in my direction, Kelsey, because I won't stand for it,' he warned in a low, ominous voice. 'I'm just as much the innocent victim of that will as you are. Joe knew I wanted complete control of McConell Real Estate—I offered to buy him out last year, for a very generous sum, I might add. He refused my offer point-blank.'

'Innocent victim!' Her eyes widened and her voice dripped with scorn. 'Don't be so ridiculous. No one in their right mind would apply that description to you. I wouldn't be surprised if you put Joe up to all of this, planted the idea in his mind so you could get your hands on the business.'

'Credit me with a little more intelligence than that.' The firm mouth twisted scornfully. 'I think I could have come up with a better and much less painful alternative than having to marry you to get them!'

That gibe cut very deep, and it silenced Kelsey effectively. Brant watched the colour flow into the porcelain-white skin with a kind of detached interest. 'Shall we go and have some lunch and discuss this like two rational adults?' he asked after a moment, in a more gentle tone.

She couldn't trust her voice not to tremble with emotion, so she just nodded.

He brought her to one of the city's most exclusive restaurants, and despite the fact that it was very busy they were shown to one of the best tables in the house almost immediately.

'Had you already booked this?' she asked him suspiciously, as the waiter left them to peruse the menu.

One dark eyebrow rose. 'Why do I get the feeling that if I say yes you are going to fly into one of your hot tempers?'

'I don't have a hot temper,' she denied calmly. 'But I hate being taken for granted.'

'So I'm finding out.' The dark eyes glittered with gentle humour. 'I guess I have a lot of things to learn about you, Kelsey McConell.'

For some unaccountable reason those words made her flush with self-conscious colour, and she looked quickly down at her menu, pretending an interest in it that wasn't really there.

She slanted a surreptitious glance over at him a few seconds later, and was relieved to find that his attention was firmly on his menu card.

The man was formidably handsome, she thought suddenly, and her stomach muscles seemed to squeeze into tight knots. The dove-grey suit sat easily on those broad shoulders, the pristine whiteness of his shirt seemed to emphasise the tanned skin and the dark hair and eyes. His eyelashes were long and dark, as well, she noticed suddenly. As she watched him they lifted, and he caught her staring at him.

'I think I—I'll have the salmon.' She said the first thing that came into her head, and then wondered awkwardly if she sounded as stupid as she felt.

'Good idea, I'll have the same.' He shut the menu with a snap and smiled at her. That smile seemed to do strange things to her blood-pressure.

She was glad that the waiter arrived at that moment for their order.

'Have you dined here before?' Brant asked casually, when they were once more left alone.

'Yes, a few times with. . .' She stumbled, for some reason suddenly loath to tell him who she had been with.

'Daniel.' He supplied the name with insouciant ease.

'Yes.' She confirmed it with a nod of her head.

'You seem to have been seeing him a lot over the last year.' His eyes moved carefully over her creamy complexion, the soft fullness of her mouth, and her eyes that were reflecting the deep jade colour of her blouse.

'A fair bit, yes.' Her answer was deliberately non-committal, and she could feel her mood swinging towards the defensive.

'Are you serious about him?' The question was asked casually enough, yet there was something about the way he was watching her that made her feel very uneasy.

'I don't think that is any of your business, Brant.' Her reply was sharper than she had intended, but she didn't try to soften it as she met his eyes across the table.

'You know why I'm asking, Kelsey.' The low-pitched voice made her nerves quiver. She didn't dare to contemplate what had prompted his sudden interest.

Their wine arrived, and Brant tasted it, then signalled for the waiter to leave them so that he could pour it himself.

'Well?' his deep voice probed as he leaned across to fill her glass, and she knew that he wasn't about to let the subject drop.

She sighed. 'I suppose you are asking all of these questions because of my grandfather's will?'

'That is what we have come to discuss,' he said drily.

'You are not proposing that we actually consider what is in that will, are you?' Her choice of wording was unfortunate—she realised that as soon as she had spoken, and her skin burned with embarrassed warmth.

He watched the glow of colour in her cheeks with wry amusement. 'I suppose that is what I'm proposing.' He gave deliberate emphasis to the word that was causing her so much discomfiture. 'Marriage could be a very lucrative proposition for us both. I don't think that you should dismiss it before you have thought it through properly.'

She had been in the process of sipping her wine and it seemed to stick somewhere in her throat at those cold words. 'Good grief, you sound as if you're talking about a business merger, not the rest of our lives!' Her voice sounded as shocked as she felt.

He shrugged. 'I'm merely being practical. I want control of McConell Real Estate, and I know that you would like to be involved in the business. I've thought it through clearly and I can see many advantages for us both if we follow this through and get married. I don't expect you to see it like that right away; I know some women tend to view things like this through a haze of emotionalism. But given time I'm sure you'll see the sense of it—you're a far-sighted and intelligent woman.'

Kelsey could hardly believe that she was hearing this;

she opened her mouth to say something, but no words came out. She wondered grimly if she was in shock, and swung her glance away from the cool, impassive face to stare out across the restaurant, hoping to gain a calmer perspective on things.

Couples sat at the intimate booths, their relaxed conversations mingling with the quiet, romantic music that was playing in the background. For a moment she found herself wondering what they would be talking about—normal things presumably, like an afternoon shopping, where they were going to spend the evening, and how much they loved each other. She wondered if any of them would glance over at them and guess that the handsome man who sat opposite to her had just proposed marriage on the grounds that it would be a lucrative venture. She could feel sudden hysterical laughter bubbling up inside her, and as it got closer towards the surface it seemed to change subtly, so that she wasn't sure if she wanted to laugh or cry. She reached for her wine glass and tried to drown the emotions by finishing the intoxicating liquid in one swallow.

'I don't expect you to give me an answer straight away, Kelsey,' he continued smoothly. 'Take your time and think it through.'

'You're all heart,' she murmured acidly.

He lifted his glass in a mocking salute.

Their first course arrived at that moment, and Kelsey stared down at the seafood in front of her and was filled with a wild desire to hurl the carefully arranged culinary delight at the infuriating face opposite.

'So how long have you known about the terms of my grandfather's will?' she asked, with icy disdain.

'Since about a week before he died.' Brant leaned across and refilled her glass. 'I was sitting next to his hospital bed talking about business, trying to keep him up-to-date on everything, when suddenly he cut across me and told me that more than anything else in the world he would like to see me marrying his grand-daughter.'

Kelsey bit down on the softness of her lip. She wasn't exactly surprised by this revelation—she had known her grandfather's thoughts on this subject for some time. 'You should have tried to talk some sense into him,' she muttered caustically.

His mouth slanted in a lop-sided grin. 'Have you ever tried to change Joe McConell's mind once it was made up?'

For a second a clear picture of her grandfather's cantankerous, stubborn face drifted into her mind, and a soft smile lit her features. She had loved that bull-headed old man so much.

'Exactly.' Brant took her expression as read. 'But anyway, the more time I have had to think about it, the more I have come to realise how wise his idea was.'

'For *you*, maybe—*you* stand to gain a hell of a lot if you marry me. Complete control of McConell Real Estate is no mean thing.' She toyed with the food in front of her, knowing that she couldn't eat a thing. Her insides were churning in chaotic disarray.

'And you will have financial security for the rest of your life,' he told her succinctly.

'I'll have that anyway,' she said with quiet dignity. 'If the shares are sold the money will be put into a trust fund for me.'

He laughed. 'And what you will receive each year will be a pittance compared to what you could have with me. Plus you will have no say whatsoever in the running of McConell Real Estate; it will have passed out of your family forever.'

Kelsey swallowed hard on a lump in her throat. How could her grandfather ever have drawn up such a will? How could he in all conscience have placed her in this position? He had known how much that business had meant to her, how hard she had pleaded for just a few shares in it. To her, McConell Real Estate was a link

with the past, to a father who was just a shadowy
memory. He had loved running that business; being a
part of it would have made her feel closer to him,
somehow. Just as working at Harcourt McConell had
made her feel closer to her grandfather. Joe McConell
had loved her in his own way, she knew; but he had had
very little time for her. Perhaps, in a way, she had
thought that being a successful lawyer would have gained
his approval, his respect, and that after a while she would
have earned a place in McConell Real Estate.

The waiter cleared away Kelsey's untouched food and
placed their main course in front of them. Somewhere in
the background she could hear a man's voice singing
about how love changed everything. Kelsey didn't even
bother to pick up her knife and fork, but reached instead
for her wine glass.

'Would you really lock yourself into a loveless marriage just for the sake of a business?' Her eyes looked an
impossibly deep shade of green as she stared across at
him.

The firm mouth tightened imperceptibly. 'I'm thirty-
seven years of age, Kelsey. I think I've left the starry-
eyed emotionalism of youth and become a little more
realistic over the years. At least, I hope I have.' He gave
her a grim smile. 'I think we could be happy together, if
that is what's worrying you. We have a lot in common, a
mutual interest in the business, and you are a desirable
woman. What more could I want?'

What more indeed? she wondered dully. At least he
thought that she was desirable; that was a little better
than intelligent and far-sighted, as far as adjectives in a
marriage proposal were concerned.

'But then, you have had your moment of starry-eyed
emotionalism,' Kelsey murmured reflectively. 'You've
been married before. I suppose you married her for more
conventional reasons than you have in mind this time?'
She lifted her wine glass and watched him carefully over
its crystal rim.

His eyes darkened slightly, but apart from that there was no other change in the cool features. 'My reasons for marrying Francesca were entirely different,' he conceded with a harsh edge to his voice, and she had the distinct impression that he was not comfortable on this subject.

Some part of her wouldn't let it drop, though. She had often wondered about the beautiful Francesca Harcourt. 'You married her because you were head over heels in love? Passionately wild about her?' The wine must have been having a strange effect on her because normally she would never have dared to ask such a question.

The firm mouth tightened. 'My wife has been dead for four years, Kelsey. Our relationship need not concern you.'

'You're right, it doesn't concern me.' She shrugged lightly. 'I just can't help wondering what makes a man like you tick.'

'A man like me?' He sounded vaguely amused now.

She took another sip of her wine and set it down before answering. 'You don't seem to have any soft edges. You're hard, cold and determined.' Good heavens! What was she saying? She should never have drunk that wine on an empty stomach.

One eyebrow rose, but he made no reply to that; it probably wasn't worthy of one. 'Do you want to leave?' he asked instead, his eyes moving to the untouched plate of food in front of her.

'Yes, please.' Her voice was little more than a whisper.

It was a while before they could get outside, as the head waiter detained them, anxious to find out if there had been something wrong with their meal.

'No, nothing,' Brant assured him easily, as he helped Kelsey on with her coat. 'Miss McConell is just not feeling very well.'

That wasn't exactly untrue, Kelsey thought, as they stepped out into the fresh air. She felt suddenly dizzy, and her steps faltered for a moment before Brant put a steadying arm around her waist.

For a second she allowed herself to lean against him. 'I'm sorry, Brant. I haven't eaten very much today and I probably shouldn't have drunk that wine.'

'And I probably shouldn't have let you,' he concurred, with an arrogance that immediately had her trying to draw away from him.

Let her! Just who did he think he was? 'You are not my husband yet, Brant,' she told him, with icy-cool firmness. 'And even if you were you couldn't dictate to me.'

'No,' he agreed smoothly. 'But I'd probably have fun trying.' The lazy amusement in his voice made her tug with renewed strength against the arm that encircled her, but her efforts were futile against his superior strength.

Only when they reached the sleek lines of the white Rolls Royce did he relax his hold, and then it was to turn her around so that she was facing him. 'I'm glad that you added the word "yet",' he murmured softly. 'It gives me room to hope.' There was no hint of amusement now in the stern face that stared down at her. She made to move her head away from that piercing gaze, but he lifted one hand and captured her chin firmly so that she was forced to look upwards. The cool touch of his fingers against her skin sent shivers running through her.

His nearness was unsettling. She could smell the elusive, warm tangy scent of his cologne. His skin had the rugged healthy glow of a man who likes to spend time outdoors. Her eyes were irresistibly drawn to the firmness of his mouth. He had an interesting mouth, she thought hazily, strong and determined yet very sensual. It was also a little too close for comfort, she realised suddenly. Her dark eyelashes fluttered downwards, shielding her eyes from his, and her breath caught in her throat as his hand moved upwards to trail through the silky length of her hair in a light caress.

Then, abruptly, he was relinquishing his hold on her and reaching to open the car door. 'We'd better get in before it starts to rain again.'

'Yes.' Her voice wobbled precariously and she sank down into the softly upholstered seat, her heart beating a crazy tattoo. For one wild moment she had thought that he was going to kiss her!

'Are you staying at your grandfather's house, or are you back at your apartment?' Brant asked casually as he settled himself behind the steering-wheel. Obviously their closeness had not had the same effect upon him, she noticed with rancour.

'I moved back to my apartment after they took grandfather into hospital.' For a moment her mind moved back to the weeks she had spent at her grandfather's house trying to look after him. It had been a period of great anxiety; Joe McConell had not been the easiest of patients. The stress of that situation, plus the trauma of his death, had taken their toll on Kelsey. She had lost far too much weight, and she felt at a very low ebb.

'You've missed the turn-off for the office,' she noticed absently.

'That's because I'm not taking you back to the office,' he said calmly. 'I'm taking you home.'

'Why on earth are you doing that? I've got stacks of work to wade through.'

He shot her a plainly mordant look, and her anger crumbled. He was probably right—she was in no fit state to return to the mountain of work on her desk today.

They didn't speak again until Brant pulled the car up in the smart residential area where she lived.

'I don't want you to come back to the office until next week,' he ordered abruptly, making her hackles rise with indignation—but she made no reply. 'Do you feel up to going to George's retirement party on Saturday?'

'I'm not an invalid, Brant.' She bit the words out crossly. 'I think I can just about manage to go to a party.'

At the same time as she made the sarcastic reply she was wondering if he was inviting her as his date.

'Well, I'll see you there, then,' he said casually. 'Will you give some thought to my proposal, Kelsey?'

Her anger flared at this cavalier attitude. Who the hell did he think he was? 'What proposal was that?' She flung her head back towards him, her eyes glistening. 'Do you mean that business proposition?' she finished, with biting sarcasm.

'You know what I mean,' he replied calmly but his dark eyes narrowed somewhat.

She shrugged. 'I might give it a thought. Then, on the other hand, I might be too busy deciding on whether I should break my grandfather's will.' She met his eyes with a supremely confident look. 'I could do it, you know. I could take this case to court and win.'

'You might,' he conceded, and to her annoyance he didn't look in the slightest bit worried. 'But it will be a risk. It will cause a big scandal, you'll probably besmirch your grandfather's name, and at the end of the day after all that you might not win.'

'But then again I might,' she persisted. 'Hadock versus Rollins, for instance. The jury found for the plaintiff. The will was broken.'

Brant nodded drily. 'And what will you plead? That Joe McConell was incompetent, or——'

'I don't know yet,' she cut across him, her voice shaking at the very thought of doing that to her grand-father. 'As I said before, I've got a lot to think about, and your. . .your business proposition is on the bottom of the list. So don't hold your breath.'

'OK, I won't hold my breath,' he answered in a dry voice. 'But I know you're not going to take this to court. So the next best thing is to think about my offer.'

'The next best thing is to forget about it all and get on with my life,' she answered, and with a wry kind of satisfaction she got out of the car. Let him stew on that for a while! Closing the door with a slam, she ran up the steps to her front door and, without waiting to watch him drive away, she let herself in.

It was only when she was safely inside that her show of bravado disappeared, and she leaned weakly back against the door-frame. Breaking her grandfather's will was something she knew was theoretically possible, but Brant was right—she knew that she wouldn't be able to do it. Not only would she feel totally humiliated if its contents became public knowledge, but she couldn't go against her grandfather's last wishes so blatantly.

What she should do was to forget about McConell Real Estate, forget the will; but that wasn't so easy, and she knew that she would give more than a passing thought to Brant's proposal—not for the mercenary reasons that he had in mind. There was no way she could marry somebody for money or power. She could only give herself to someone if she truly loved them, and there was the crux of her problem, because she had been more than a little in love with Brant Harcourt since she had first set eyes on him.

CHAPTER THREE

'WE MISSED you at work this week, darling.'

'Thanks, Daniel, but I'm surprised that you noticed my absence. I believe things have been very hectic in there.' Kelsey settled herself back into her armchair, welcoming the deep husky tone that broke the silence of her apartment.

'Aren't they always? But of course we missed you. Is everything all right with you, Kel?'

'Yes, I just needed some extra time off,' she assured the voice at the other end of the phone.

'Ah!' he drawled, with dramatic emphasis. 'I'd almost forgotten. They read your grandfather's will last Tuesday, didn't they?'

'Yes,' Kelsey answered shortly. She didn't believe for one moment that Daniel had forgotten about that particular thing. Speculation at the office was probably rife by now. She steeled herself for the inevitable questions, but surprisingly none came.

'Just rang to see if you still wanted to accompany me to this party tonight?' he asked smoothly.

'To be honest with you, Daniel, I have been wrestling with my conscience. I'm not really in the mood for a party tonight, yet I don't think I should miss something as important as George's retirement. He was Joe's oldest friend, and he has been with the company for as long as I can remember.'

'Yes, everything seems to be changing at Harcourt McConell, but that's life, Kel; one door closes and another opens.'

'Slams in your face, you mean?' she answered, with dry humour.

He laughed. 'Do come tonight, Kelsey. It will do you

good to mingle with everybody and have a drink. Not to mention the fact that I will never find another date at this late hour.'

Now it was her turn to laugh. 'That, Daniel Marsden, is a downright lie. Your little black book is filled with women who would go out with you at a moment's notice, and you know it. However, as you have requested the pleasure of my company so charmingly, I can hardly refuse, can I?'

'That's my girl!' She could hear the smile in his voice. 'I'll pick you up at eight.'

Kelsey knew that she had made the right decision to attend the party the moment she put the phone down. For once she didn't want to be alone, and it probably would do her good to mix among her colleagues and enjoy some light-hearted conversation. She tried to cast the knowledge that Brant would be there among that crowd right to the back of her mind, but she couldn't help wondering who his date for the evening would be. She remembered the glamorous redhead who had been on his arm at the last function they had attended; would she still be on the scene?

It was typical of Brant's cold, analytical character that he could propose marriage to her and then in the same week bring another woman as his date to a party. It made it clearer than any words could have that Brant considered marriage to her as a cold-blooded business arrangement only. Somewhere deep inside a raw ache started to eat away at her. She glanced across the luxuriously furnished room to where her grandfather's portrait hung above the Adam fireplace. 'How could you do this to me?' she whispered aloud.

Her gaze locked on the determined look in the old man's green eyes. He had never made any secret of the fact that he thought Brant Harcourt would be an eminently suitable husband for her. She remembered the sparkle in his eyes the day that he had introduced them in his office, and then soon afterwards how he had sent her around to Brant's house on the pretext of delivering some documents.

She had known that there was nothing of importance in those papers, had been well aware that they could have waited for him to come into the office on Monday morning. But her grandfather had been so adamant about it that she had given in and taken them. Even thinking about that incident made her blood-pressure start to rise.

She had rung the bell several times and there had been no reply, yet Brant's silver-blue Aston Martin had been sitting in the drive, so she hadn't thought that he would be far away. On impulse she had stepped around the side of the house and peered through the nearest window. To this day she didn't know what had possessed her to do such a thing; it wasn't something that she would normally have dreamt of doing.

The sight that had met her eyes was imprinted on her memory. Brant had been standing locked in a passionate embrace with an incredibly beautiful brunette. One hand had rested lightly on her slender waist; the other was lifting the long luxuriant hair so that his lips could blaze a tormenting trail over smooth bare shoulders. His eyes had lifted at that moment and they had immediately come to rest on Kelsey's crimson face.

She had been mortified, had felt like some sort of peeping Tom. She had almost fallen over in her haste to get away from the place. Unfortunately, Brant had been too quick for her and had opened the front door before she had had a chance to get to her car.

'Can I do anything for you, Miss McConell?' he had asked with wry amusement, which for some reason made her blood start to boil.

'I just called to make sure you got these.' She had pushed the documents into his hands, cursing her grandfather, cursing the fact that those documents were just trivia and that he would know that there was no real reason for her coming out here. 'I'm sorry if I disturbed you,' she managed to say lamely.

'That's all right.' The dark eyes had held a mocking light. 'You'll understand if I don't invite you in?'

Kelsey had understood all right. She had driven back to her apartment with a speed that would have burnt the tar. It was only then that she had started to realise that all the feelings of antagonism and resentment that she had been feeling towards Brant since he had come into the business a few months before had just been a smokescreen for other much deeper feelings—that she was jealous as could be of that beautiful brunette.

Her grandfather had hardly been able to wait for her to get into the office the following morning before broaching the subject of her visit to Brant's house. 'How did you get on?' He made no attempt to hide his interest.

'With what?' She was deliberately obtuse.

'With Brant, of course.'

'I gave him the document, he thanked me. Then I came home.' Her tone told him very clearly to back off, but he ignored that.

'He didn't invite you in?'

'No, he was otherwise occupied with his girlfriend.'

She allowed more emotion that she had intended to show in her voice, and her grandfather was nothing if not perceptive.

'A little thing like that shouldn't have thrown you,' he said with a smile. 'I've never known you not to go after something you want with positive determination.'

What Joe McConell had said was true. If she wanted something she did pursue it. But her career, her job at Harcourt McConell, even moving into her own apartment—all those things were slightly different from pursuing a man. Her confidence in that area was definitely shaky. 'There's no point anyway,' she muttered crossly. 'I told you, he has a girlfriend.'

Joe McConell gave a derisive snort. 'There will be nothing serious about that.'

The certainty in the old man's voice made her frown. 'How on earth do you know if it's serious or not?'

'Because I have inside information on Brant Harcourt,' Joe answered smugly. 'I know his late wife's father very well indeed. He's a judge on the high-court circuit. He told me only the other day that Brant had not got over Francesca's death yet, and it has been nearly three years. He was crazy about her, you know, went into a total decline after her death.'

'Yes, well, that's really none of our business,' Kelsey murmured quietly.

'Of course it's our business—where is your compassion, Kelsey?' The green eyes fixed firmly on to her. 'The poor man is apparently still suffering from grief and he's all alone in that large house of his. I think we should start inviting him out for dinner. We could throw a small dinner party at my house at the weekend.'

Kelsey shook her head. 'No, Grandfather, and don't start interfering.'

'What's interfering about inviting someone for dinner? I can't see the harm in it,' Joe persisted stubbornly. 'Go and ask him, Kelsey. I'm sure it would mean a lot to him.'

And so it was that Kelsey found herself in Brant's office a few minutes later.

'What can I do for you, Miss McConell?' His voice was crisp, and he hardly bothered to look up from the papers that he was studying. He looked every inch the successful lawyer in a dark business suit, his face set in a seriously determined expression as he drew a pen across a page which obviously irritated him.

For a moment Kelsey felt extremely foolish as she remembered how she had been swayed by her grandfather's opinion that Brant was a lonely man. Ridiculous!

'Kelsey, I'm an extremely busy man.' Hard eyes swept over her slim figure in the smart navy blue suit. His use of her Christian name threw her for a moment, and she didn't answer immediately.

'If it's about the position for junior partner, then I'm afraid you are wasting your time as well as mine. The post has already been offered elsewhere.'

Disappointment flowed in icy waves right through her, but also cold anger at the way this man was talking to her. Just who did he think he was? 'I already know about that; my grandfather informed me.' It was a downright lie—Joe had not bothered to mention it at all—but somehow saying that made her feel as if she was saving face. 'I came to invite you for dinner one night this week——'

'Sorry, I'm busy.' He bent his head back to his work. 'You wouldn't get around me that way, anyhow. The decision has already been made. You can't expect to be given special preference because you are Joe McConell's granddaughter—you may have had it in the past, but I'm afraid it's a different story now that I have joint control of the business.'

The harsh words completely took her breath away; she could hardly believe her ears! 'How dare you speak to me like that? I don't expect any special privileges, nor have I ever had them.'

'No?' The look he levelled at her was frankly disbelieving. 'Well, thank you for the dinner invitation, Miss McConell, but, as I said, I'm very busy.'

Even thinking about that conversation now made her hands clench into tight fists. Lord, that man could be such an arrogant swine! Yet when he smiled at her, when he spoke to her in that gentle deep tone that he used towards her these days, she could feel every bone in her body start to melt.

She got up from her chair with a sigh. 'You've gone too far this time, Joe McConell,' she muttered at the portrait on the way past. 'Brant doesn't really want me, he doesn't even like me. What sort of marriage would that be, for heaven's sake?' With a shake of her head she went upstairs to start preparing for the evening ahead.

Her bedroom was like the rest of her apartment, tastefully and elegantly furnished. The colour theme, a pleasing blend of misty grey and pale pink, was carried through into the en suite bathroom, and it was towards this room that Kelsey headed now to turn on the forceful jet of the shower.

She was proud of her home because apart from the deposit for it, which had been a twenty-first birthday present from her grandfather, she had attained it by her own hard work. It pleased that proud independent streak inside her to look around and know that the moneyed elegance that surrounded her was entirely due to her own efforts.

She felt more like going out after she had had her shower, and she was actually starting to look forward to the evening as she stepped back into her bedroom.

Sitting at her dressing-table, she blow-dried her hair back into its usual silky, sophisticated style. Then she leaned across towards her stereo system to switch on a compact disc. The hauntingly romantic music of Luther Vandross filled the room, and Kelsey smiled to herself as she stepped into silk underwear and then applied the minimum of make-up to her pale delicate features. Brant would probably have a fit if he knew that she liked to listen to such blatantly romantic ballads. In all likelihood he would dismiss such music as unrealistic drivel.

Almost as if in an act of defiance, she turned the volume on the stereo up as she passed en route to her wardrobe. Her fingers flicked along the rows of clothes, lingering indecisively on silk, then cashmere, before coming to rest on a dress that was completely different from her usual style of smartly efficient clothes—this was flagrantly and extravagantly romantic. With a sudden sparkle in her emerald-green eyes, she pulled it out.

It was only when she was seated in the front seat of Daniel's sleek sports car that she started to have second thoughts about the dress. The thing was that there was very little of it. It plunged at the back and at the front, and clung lovingly to her slender figure, showing every curve to perfection. It wouldn't have been quite so bad if she had worn a necklace to take the attention away from where the sea-green silk curved daringly at her breast.

'Well, anyway, I didn't think we stood a hope in heaven of winning that case——' Daniel was busy relating a trial that had finished earlier that week '—but somehow Brant managed to do it. The prosecution didn't know what had hit them; they obviously thought that it was going to be an easy victory for them. Then just at the right moment Brant introduced a vital piece of evidence! Honestly, Kel, his timing was nothing short of brilliant.' There was a note of awed respect in the younger man's voice. 'I'd hate to come up against Brant in a court of law—the man is positively lethal.'

'You can say that again,' Kelsey muttered in an undertone, as she stared out at the darkened streets lit by bright neon lights.

'No wonder Joe McConell was so keen to get him as his partner,' Daniel continued smoothly, oblivious to the fact that his companion was starting to clench her hands.

'I always thought that George Wright would have been a better choice,' she replied stiffly, wishing that he would drop the subject of Brant Harcourt—she would like to forget that man's very existence this evening.

'You're joking!' Daniel turned startled eyes on her. 'George is far too old. It's his retirement party tonight, remember?'

'He might not be retiring if he had been offered the partnership,' Kelsey maintained stubbornly.

Daniel shook his head in disagreement. 'Anyway, George would never have had the money to have bought in in such a big way. He's a good attorney, but he is not in Brant's league financially or professionally.' He took his eyes from the busy road for a second to slant another look at her. 'Are you trying to tell me that you don't care very much for Brant?'

She shrugged slim shoulders in a deliberately careless way. 'He's all right.'

Daniel gave a deep laugh. 'You've got to be the only woman in Toronto who thinks that Brant Harcourt is just all right. He has to be the most eligible bachelor in the city. Apart from me, of course,' he added with a grin.

'You're well out of his league.' She mimicked his earlier words in a teasing way.

'I hope that is meant as a compliment, Miss McConell.' He pulled the car to a standstill outside the Majestic hotel, which had been the venue for a lot of the company's functions just lately. He turned to look at her, the laughing glint in his eyes belying the stern tone of his voice.

'But of course.' She sounded amazed that he would think otherwise, and they both laughed.

'Tormenting minx!' He leaned across to kiss her lips lightly, and then seemed to change his mind about pulling away, and deepened the caress.

Kelsey was no stranger to Daniel's kisses. They were never serious and she made sure that they never led anywhere. She was well aware that Daniel was a compulsive womaniser, that he had a different woman for every night of the week, and it didn't bother her at all. She valued Daniel's friendship above everything else.

'Why, here's Brant!' Daniel murmured as he straightened. Kelsey glanced up to see the familiar white Rolls-Royce with its personalised number plates drawing up in front of them. As she watched, Brant got out and went around to the passenger side of the car to open the door. For a moment she was so fascinated by those incredibly handsome good looks, accentuated by dark evening clothes, that she didn't immediately notice the woman he was politely helping from the car.

'Well, well, if it isn't our dear Susanna Winters,' Daniel breathed in surprise.

Kelsey's eyes moved immediately to the beautiful blonde who was now tucking her arm in a proprietorial manner through Brant's.

She frowned, and her heart seemed to plunge painfully down. 'I didn't know Susanna was seeing Brant.' Her voice had a strange husky note to it.'

'Neither did I. She'll have cause for double celebration tonight.'

'What do you mean?' Kelsey tore her eyes away from the slender figure in the glittering white evening dress to look back at Daniel.

'Her divorce came through yesterday. I managed to get her a prime chunk of real estate plus an impressive financial settlement. I imagine she's feeling on top of the world with all that and the man of her dreams on her arm,' he finished drily.

'Yes, I imagine so,' Kelsey echoed in a hollow tone. She had never liked Susanna Winters, even though she was a fellow lawyer with the company, and a similar age to herself. Kelsey had always thought her to be a very cold and calculating type. Brant would probably be the ideal partner for her, she thought bitterly.

'I wonder if they saw us?' she murmured now, returning her glance to where the couple were disappearing through the swing doors into the brightly lit foyer.

'Probably—Brant doesn't miss much,' Daniel grinned.

Kelsey found herself hoping that he had witnessed that kiss of a moment ago. Not that it would have jogged any emotional feelings in that steel-encased heart of his, but it might have made him worry about getting the McConell shares—might make him regret his decision to invite Susanna to this party instead of her. She wished fervently that Brant was now worried sick about his precious shares.

'Well, I suppose we should go in and join the fun.'

Daniel waited for the doorman to get into Brant's car
and drive it away for parking before he moved his own
car up a space, ready for another attendant to come and
park it for him.

The large function suite on the top floor was crowded
with Harcourt McConell employees. As always, the
company had spared no expense in its choice of venue.
The Majestic's function-rooms were the most luxurious
in town. There were thick red carpets, and white kid-
leather seats placed at strategical points so that people
could enjoy an intimate conversation and the panoramic
view out over the glittering lights of the city. A band
played unobtrusively in the background a soothing
medley of Glenn Miller music.

Despite the crowds, Kelsey's eyes went directly to
Brant's tall powerful figure the moment they entered the
room. A man who looked more confident and composed
would be hard to find, she thought grimly, as she
watched him throw back his head and laugh at some
remark that Susanna had made. So much for his worrying about her and the shares! Was he really so self-
assured that he believed she would accept his proposal
despite Susanna, despite Daniel, and of course the fact
that he had made no attempt to sweet-talk her into
accepting? She had never met anyone quite so sure of
himself in her life before. It made her want to scream
with frustration, and in that moment she longed to be
able to hurt him the way he was hurting her, standing
with his arm around Susanna's tiny waist. But how could
you hurt a man who had no feelings? She had the
impression that even if she told him here and now that
she had no intention of letting him get his hands on the
McConell shares that he would shrug those broad
shoulders and take the news in his stride.

'Kelsey, how lovely to see you!' George Wright came
across to clasp her hand warmly. 'You look stunning,
my dear.' Bright blue eyes sparkled in an age-lined face.

'If I was thirty years younger I would be giving Brant Harcourt some real competition.'

Kelsey frowned in perplexity. 'Thank you, George, but actually I'm here with Daniel.' She looked around for her escort and noticed that he was behind her at the bar, getting them a drink.

'Ah, yes.' George sounded slightly uncomfortable for a moment.

Kelsey turned her attention back to the older man, a horrible suspicion growing in her mind. Did George Wright know about the terms of her grandfather's will? She would die of embarrassment if it had somehow become public knowledge. She had been so relieved that Harold was handling the will, because he had no connection with Harcourt McConell except for the fact that he was an old acquaintance of her grandfather's.

Aware that Kelsey was looking more than a little horrified, George shrugged apologetically. 'Sorry, honey, but Joe never made any secret of the fact that he thought that you two were perfect for each other. I guess I heard it so many times that I automatically tend to think of you and Brant as a couple.'

'He did seem to have a bit of a fixation about it,' Kelsey agreed drily, but she started to relax again. 'He was always trying to throw us together.' Even now, she thought with a shiver; even after his death he wasn't giving up.

'I believe that they read Joe's will this week,' George remarked now, his face sad. 'What are you going to do with his shares in the business, Kelsey? Will you and Brant be running McConell Real Estate together?'

'I don't know, I haven't made up my mind yet.' It wasn't a lie exactly, but it wasn't the truth. Kelsey bit down on the softness of her lower lip and tried to console herself that at least he didn't know the awful facts about Joe's will—that the only partnership that her grandfather wanted for her was marriage.

'If you want some advice on the subject, Kelsey, then

I think you should sell your McConell shares,' George offered tentatively. 'You're much too young for all that responsibility. I'm sure Brant would offer you top price, and the company would flourish if he had complete control.'

'I'm sure it would,' Kelsey muttered. But I can't sell them to any one person, she thought miserably. All she could do was stand by and let the company be split into little pieces, or she could take them to Brant like some sort of Victorian dowry. She tried to omit the last option from her mind; how could she even consider such a thing? It was unthinkable to offer yourself as part of some package deal to a man who cared nothing at all for you.

Unconsciously, her eyes sought Brant across the room; he was talking to his secretary and a group of young girls from the typing pool. They all looked as if they were hanging on his every word, as if whatever he was telling them was of earth-shattering importance. A shaft of annoyance hit her. Everybody held Brant in such high esteem, bowed and scraped if he so much as glanced at them. She had noticed in particular the way the girls in the typing pool practically swooned every time that he walked by. She couldn't blame them—he had a similar effect on her, the only difference being that she had too much pride to let it show. It was really little wonder that the man was so insufferably arrogant.

'Sorry I was so long.' Daniel held out a glass of wine to her and then handed George a drink. 'Here's to your retirement,' he said with a grin. 'What are you planning to do with yourself now?'

'A bit of fishing, spend more time with the grand-children.' George laughed. 'I think I'm going to be pretty busy.'

'Not too busy to pay us a visit now and again, I hope.' Brant's deep voice interrupted them from behind, sending a shiver down Kelsey's spine. Deliberately, she didn't turn her head to look at him, but kept her eyes firmly on George's face.

'No, I'll never be that busy, Brant.' There was a tinge of regret in the old man's voice now. 'I'm going to miss you all a great deal.'

'We'll miss you as well.' Kelsey spoke softly. 'Things won't be the same.'

'I don't suppose that you will have much time for sentiment once you are installed in charge of McConell Real Estate,' Susanna Winters cut in, a sharp edge in her silvery voice.

'What makes you think I'll be in charge?' Kelsey turned to look at the other woman now, noting with rising irritation how she was still clinging to Brant's arm. The slender body in the white designer dress pressed close against Brant's dark suit.

'Well, I suppose it goes without saying—I mean, we all know that you are going to get the McConell shares.' Susanna gave her a sickly-sweet smile from poppy-red lips. 'It must be wonderful to have everything in life handed to you on a silver platter.' The words were lightly spiced with envy, yet Kelsey had the feeling that there was more malice than jealousy in them. For some reason the woman was deliberately trying to make her look bad.

'Indeed it must,' she agreed, keeping her tone carefully light. 'But as I have never had anything handed to me I wouldn't know.'

'Now that I find hard to believe!' Susanna trailed a hand over the short, sophisticated style of her blonde hair in a gesture that was more for effect than anything else. 'I mean, Joe must have had your name down at law school when you were ten and he probably had your name put on your office door at around the same time.' She finished on a low silvery laugh.

'Actually I won a scholarship into law school,' Kelsey informed her succinctly. 'And Joe, as you seem fond of calling him these days——' she gave a sweet smile to belie the dig that when he was alive Susanna would never

have dared to call her grandfather anything other than
Mr McConell '—wanted me to take up something he
thought more advantageous for a woman, namely the art
of good cuisine.' She slanted a glance up at Brant to find
that he was watching her, a glimmer of amusement
in his dark eyes. The fact that he was deriving enter-
tainment from their exchange angered her more than
Susanna's stupid remarks, and her green eyes took on a
frosty glitter as they held his.

For some reason this served only to amuse him
further, and then his eyes moved with lazy interest down
over the curves of her body, making her painfully aware
of how frivolous the frothy silk dress was and how little
it covered. 'Would you like to dance, Kelsey?'

For a moment she thought that she had misheard that
softly spoken invitation, and she could only stare up at
him blankly. Then he was reaching over for her arm, a
smile lighting the cool dark features.

The thought of refusal ran fleetingly through her
mind. . .very fleetingly. Then, with a polite smile at the
people around them, she allowed him to lead her to the
small dance-floor. She tried to tell herself that she had
accepted just to see the look of annoyance on Susanna
Winters' face, but in reality she knew that she hadn't
even noticed what expression the girl's face had taken.
All she had noticed was Brant's powerfully handsome
figure in the dark suit, those eyes that seemed to see into
her soul, and the way his lips were curved in a firm but
somehow inviting way.

A tremble ran through her entire body as he took her
into his arms and held her close. She allowed herself to
relax against him, her honey-gold hair against his broad
chest as she breathed in the heady elusive aroma that
was unmistakably Brant Harcourt.

The band was playing the hauntingly romantic melody
of 'Stranger on the Shore', and maybe it was that, or
maybe it was the way Brant's hand was resting against

the smooth bare skin of her back, but suddenly she wanted to melt against him and never let him go.

'You handled Susanna very well.' The cool words did nothing to break the spell that held her. His voice sounded like deep velvet with her head resting so close, and she could hear the heavy beat of his heart against her ear.

'Brant.' His name sounded like a sigh on her lips. 'Do you know that this is the first time that you have ever asked me to dance?'

'Is it?' He sounded vaguely amused now. 'I had no idea that you kept track of such things!'

Kelsey bit down on her bottom lip, upset to find that she was hurt more than angered by his sarcastic humour. It was ridiculous how easily he was able to hurt her; it made her feel foolish and also more shockingly aware of just how vulnerable she was where he was concerned.

'Have you given my proposal any more thought?' he asked coolly.

She shook her head, not trusting herself to rational speech.

'Well, maybe you could spare me a little thought now.' His voice had a slight husky quality in it as he trailed his hand over her back and then tangled his fingers into her long silk hair. 'Did I tell you, by the way, that you look very sexy in that dress?'

The touch of his fingers and those words made her blood race like molten lava through her veins. Furious with herself and with him, she drew herself stiffly away from the warmth of his body and glared up at him, her eyes gleaming like brightly polished jewels. 'If you think that you will get around me with a few token compliments, then you're way off course. I don't know how you have the nerve to talk to me about marriage when your date for the evening is standing only a few feet away.' Her low voice trembled slightly with the force of her emotions. 'Sometimes I think that you must have a heart made out of granite—that you have no feelings whatsoever.'

He smiled down at her, but the jet-dark eyes were cool. 'Susanna knows exactly where she stands with me, Kelsey; I never pretend to be something I'm not. I don't whisper passionate endearments or make promises that I have no intention of keeping. I am always honest with women. If that makes me seem cold and unfeeling, then that's their problem.'

'Well, I for one don't want your brand of honesty.' Her voice caught on a lump in her throat and she tried to turn her eyes away from the compelling intensity of his gaze, but he wouldn't let her; his fingers tightened in her hair, forcing her to look up at him.

'You would like me to act more like Daniel, is that it?' His voice was as sharp and as cutting as ice. 'You want me to declare undying love and utter meaningless tender words in order to get what I want? You do realise that where women are concerned Daniel Marsden does not have a sincere bone in his body?' One dark eyebrow rose sardonically. 'Is that what turns you on, Kelsey? Is that the veneer that you would like me to attain for you? Would that make me a more feeling, caring person in your eyes?'

'I don't want anything from you.' Her voice was low and tremulous, but she held his eyes bravely.

'Liar.' He breathed the word softly as he lowered his lips towards hers.

A rush of electric feeling surged through her, and her eyes widened with surprise at the realisation that he was about to kiss her, right here in front of everyone! She should have made some effort to turn her head away, but she did nothing, just waited with a kind of breathless anticipation.

His mouth was tormentingly light, sending tingling darts of pure electric sensation down into the very depths of her soul, making her crave for some more, like a drug that once tasted drove you out of your mind with need.

She deepened the kiss of her own volition, heedless of the people around them, of everything except the sweet sensation of being close to Brant. As soon as he tasted the strength of her response he moved her gently away.

'That's what you want, Kelsey,' he murmured softly. 'And it has lain between us since the first moment we looked into each other's eyes.'

She stared up at him, wanting desperately to be able to deny those words; but how could she deny a truth that was so glaringly obvious? It had just been one little kiss, but her whole heart had been poured into it. Her eyes clouded with pain and humiliation, and quickly she tore herself away from him and pushed her way through the crowds. She was unaware of the interested eyes that turned to watch her, or the fact that Brant was close on her heels. Her only thought at that moment was to get away, to go somewhere private and cry bitter tears of shame.

'Kelsey!' His deep voice halted her in the long corridors outside the function-room.

'Go away, Brant. You've succeeded in making me look and feel enough of a fool for one evening.' Her voice was clear and steady, but she didn't dare to turn and look at him. Keeping her head held high she started to walk towards the lifts. He fell in step beside her.

'Since when has it been considered foolish to be attracted to someone?' he asked her in a light, teasing tone.

'Since the day we met.' She bit through clenched teeth. 'I knew then that I should keep my distance. That if I came anywhere near you I would get badly burned.'

'Funny, but I thought exactly the same thing,' he murmured reflectingly.

Those words stopped her in her tracks and she turned towards him in surprise. 'You did?' she asked in disbelief.

Amusement flared briefly in those dark eyes before he

nodded seriously. 'But I'm willing to risk the fire now if you are.'

If that look of sardonic amusement hadn't briefly crossed his features she might have been taken in. 'Now that you have so much to gain, you mean?' she asked, in a derisive tone.

'We both have a lot to gain, Kelsey.' His voice was dangerously soft.

She shook her head. 'I don't think I will be gaining very much by tying myself to a man who has no feelings for anything other than business. Love and romance come high on my list of priorities, Brant. I don't expect you to understand that, seeing as they don't figure anywhere at all on yours.'

'That's quite a speech,' he drawled laconically, 'and such commendable sentiments. You'll have to forgive me for finding them hard to believe; you see, I never had you pegged as the kind of girl to put hearts and flowers over and above advancement in her career.'

'But then you don't really know me, do you, Brant?' she returned sharply.

He was silent for a moment. 'Then maybe you should give me an opportunity to rectify that. How about dinner tomorrow night?'

She started to turn away from him. 'No, thank you, Brant. I've told you I'm not interested——'

His hand reached out and caught her arm in a firm grip. 'The devil you aren't,' he grated harshly. 'You've been interested in me since day one.' He pulled her back in against the hard strength of his body. 'I don't know what your game is, Kelsey—whether you're just playing hard to get, or if you're running scared—but, whichever it is, I am the one who's going to win this particular game.' He released her then, and walked with long determined strides back towards the party.

She watched him go, her heart pounding unsteadily. It took her a few moments to gather herself together. Who did Brant Harcourt think he was? He had to be the most arrogant, chauvinistic man that she had ever met. Playing hard to get—running scared—indeed! She would show him how little he bothered her.

With her head held high she made her way back to the party. As soon as she entered the room her eyes met Brant's across the sea of people, and the gleam of triumph that she saw in them made her whole body churn with apprehension. He had been expecting her to follow him back inside, she realised suddenly. Those taunting words had been a deliberate ploy to lure her back. She hated the feeling that Brant Harcourt had just manipulated her with the greatest of ease, but she was terrified by the knowledge that this was just the beginning, and Brant Harcourt always got what he wanted.

CHAPTER FOUR

'SOME more flowers have arrived for you, Kelsey.' Maggie shouldered her way through the door, her arms filled with an enormous bouquet of white roses. 'I wonder where we should put them?' The girl stood in the centre of the office and glanced around, her eyes sparkling. 'We seem to have run out of space for them.' She laughed.

Kelsey wasn't laughing. When the first bouquet had arrived at nine this morning she had been pleasantly surprised, but when they had kept on arriving at hourly intervals she had started to get annoyed. The whole building was buzzing with the news of the flowers that kept arriving, and no doubt Maggie had informed them that they were from Brant. The gossips would be having a field day with this, and heaven alone knew what Daniel would be thinking. Thankfully he hadn't noticed the way Brant had kissed her at the party, so she had not had to parry any difficult questions. But he would have to be blind not to have seen all the flowers that had floated past his door today. Kelsey didn't think that he would be jealous or anything—they didn't have that kind of a relationship—but he would be curious—very curious.

'I couldn't find any more containers to put them in either,' Maggie carried on enthusiastically. 'Should I send one of the girls out for something?'

'No,' Kelsey muttered. 'Just dump them down somewhere—anywhere,' she tacked on with exasperation, as her secretary searched for a free space. In the end the girl placed the Cellophane-wrapped flowers down in the chair opposite to Kelsey.

'I guess they will be all right there, seeing as you don't

have any more appointments today and it's nearly time for home,' she said with a grin.

'Is Brant back from court yet?' Kelsey enquired, without amusement.

'No, but he will be any time now. I'll let you know the minute he comes in.' She turned towards the door with a sigh. 'I wish someone would send me flowers like this, especially someone like Brant Harcourt. It's so romantic.'

Kelsey glared at her secretary as the latter retreated, Brant's motives for sending those flowers were coldly calculating. She wasn't fooled for one moment into thinking that there was any romantic sentiment attached to them. The thought that everyone else would be duped into thinking there was something going on between them was irritating in the extreme. With a sigh that was pure vexation she turned her attention back to the legal documents on her desk.

The intercom buzzed a few minutes later, and she looked up to see Susanna Winters standing in the outer office.

'Susanna Winters would like a word with you, Kelsey,' her secretary informed her. 'Is it all right for her to come in?'

It wasn't. Susanna was the last person that she wanted to talk to at this moment, but she could do nothing other than have her sent in.

As usual the woman looked stunning. The short blonde hairstyle was very sophisticated, her make-up perfect and the designer silk suit, which was a glorious shade of purple, was tailored to the willowy slim figure showing every little curve to its best advantage. Susanna always succeeded in making Kelsey feel incredibly gauche.

'What can I do for you, Susanna?' She forced a smile into place as she waved the woman towards the seat opposite. She couldn't have said why, but it gave her a small measure of satisfaction that her visitor had to lift the bouquet from the chair before she could sit down. The feeling faded, however, as she watched the woman blatantly lift the card that accompanied the flowers to read it. Kelsey's heart thudded nervously as her imagination ran riot over the possibilities of what could be written on that card.

'Are you going to accept?' Susanna let the bouquet drop to the floor with a thud.

'Accept what?' For a wild moment Kelsey wondered if there had been a marriage proposal written on it.

'Brant's invitation to dinner,' Susanna replied with a sharp edge of impatience in the silvery voice.

'I don't know yet.' Kelsey forced herself to relax. Of course there had been nothing personal on the card. Brant would have got his secretary to organise the sending of those flowers. She could almost see the scene now. Brant sitting behind that enormous desk, going through the morning's correspondence with his secretary. Then, when all the important business for the day was sorted, he would have said casually, 'Oh, and arrange a bouquet to be sent to Miss McConell. In fact send her one every hour and you can put an invitation to dinner on the last one at five.'

It was an effort to push those strong dark features from her mind and concentrate on the woman who sat opposite.

'I just wondered.' Susanna shrugged and leaned back into her chair, perfectly at ease.

'Was there something in particular that you wanted?' Kelsey enquired politely.

'Yes. I want to know exactly what is going on between you and Brant.'

Kelsey tried to keep her face as impassive and cool as the woman's opposite, but it was a struggle. 'I don't think that is really any of your business, Susanna.'

'Well, I disagree. You see, Brant has been dating me for a couple of months now, so I think that I have every right to ask you what your intentions are towards him.'

The silky voice was carefully modulated and in perfect control, yet Kelsey sensed that behind those cold blue eyes furious fires of temper were blazing.

'Then perhaps it should be Brant's intentions that you should be questioning,' Kelsey suggested gently. Suddenly she felt sorry for this woman and very, very angry with Brant. He really was a cold-hearted rat; at least if he wanted to start something with her he could have had the decency to finish with Susanna first. Even Daniel, with all his womanising, was not as audacious as Brant!

'I have no need to do that, Kelsey.' The words were dripping with scorn. 'I already know what Brant's intentions are towards you. He wants the McConell shares and for some reason you are refusing to sell them.'

'Really? This is all news to me.' Kelsey widened her green eyes in a guileless expression, her sympathy with the woman rapidly evaporating.

'Well, one doesn't have to be Einstein to work it out. It's patently obvious that the only interest Brant has in you is those shares. It really is very pathetic of you to hold on to them just to keep his attention. You're behaving like a fool.'

'There is an old proverb, Susanna, that says, "The fool is busy in everyone's business but his own".' Kelsey gave her a cool smile. 'Perhaps you would close the door behind you on the way out?'

The woman shrugged and rose nonchalantly to her feet. The exotic perfume that she was wearing drifted through the air, overpowering the delicate scent of flowers in the office, and making Kelsey feel slightly ill.

She turned at the door. 'Just remember, Kelsey, that *I* was the woman Brant chose to invite to last Saturday's party and *I* was the one he took home. . .back to his place.'

The door opened and then closed, leaving Kelsey seething with fury. The woman had a diabolical nerve to come in and speak to her like that! She was obviously eaten up with jealousy. Kelsey curled her hands into tight fists. She could hardly blame the woman for feeling jealous, not when the same emotion was eating away at her now. If it had been she who had spent Saturday night in Brant's arms and then discovered him sending flowers to another woman on Monday she would have been completely and utterly devastated.

The intercom buzzed on her desk. 'Brant is back from court now, Kelsey,' Maggie informed her cheerfully.

Kelsey pursed her lips and her eyes blazed with anger as she got to her feet. She had one or two choice words to say to Brant Harcourt. Lifting the bouquet of roses that Susanna had dropped to the floor, she carried it with her as she headed with determination for the elevator.

'Kelsey, honey! This is a surprise.' Brant was pouring himself a drink from the cabinet in his office as his secretary showed her in. 'Would you like to join me in a Jack Daniels, or would you prefer something else?'

'I don't want anything from you.' Kelsey flung the bouquet of roses down on to his desk, sending a few papers flurrying to the ground. 'And that includes your flowers.'

He turned to study her with lazy amusement; his eyes moved over the buttercup-yellow suit that accentuated her curvy figure so beautifully, and then came to rest on her face and the fierce sparkle in her jade-green eyes. 'You're even more beautiful when you are angry, do you know that, Kelsey?'

'More beautiful than what?' she shot back quickly. 'Susanna Winters?'

Dark eyebrows rose slightly at that. 'Ah. . .' he murmured, as if suddenly enlightened. 'I see.'

She frowned. 'I don't think that you do,' she told him caustically. 'I thought that I made myself clear when I told you on Saturday that I am not interested either in you or this ridiculous idea of marriage, and I resent your placing me in such an invidious situation today by sending me all those flowers.'

'I didn't realise that sending a few flowers was invidious, it was supposed to be romantic.' He crossed the room towards her and leaned back against his desk. Humour lit his dark eyes and he looked as if he found all of this highly entertaining. 'You did tell me that you like a little romance in your life. I gained the impression that you would not be averse to some gentle wooing.'

'Well, you gained the wrong impression,' she assured him forcefully.

'Pity, it's a long time since I had to actively pursue a woman with flowers and candy. I was kind of looking forward to it.' He grinned at her. 'I was even starting to revise my opinion of you as a hard-headed businesswoman.'

For a moment Kelsey was almost side-tracked by that; she wanted to ask him why you couldn't be a tough businesswoman and romantic as well, but that was leading her away from the reason she had come up here, and she was still boiling mad. 'I don't think there is anything remotely romantic about sending flowers to one woman while at the same time dating another who works in this very building,' she told him in no uncertain terms.

'And now we are back to Susanna Winters, I presume?' He swirled the whiskey around the crystal tumbler before taking a sip of the golden liquid. His manner was so nonchalant and relaxed, and he looked so damn attractive in the midnight blue suit, that Kelsey felt as if her blood-pressure was getting ready to explode.

'Unless you are dating other employees that I don't know about? Which quite frankly wouldn't surprise me in the least,' she returned with cutting sarcasm.

'No, there is no one else,' he replied seriously, ignoring the gibe. 'And there's no need for you to get worked up about Susanna. Sure, I've taken her out a few times and we enjoy each other's company, but that is all there is to it. There is no serious involvement and Susanna knows exactly where she stands.'

Just as I do, Kelsey thought despondently. 'And that is supposed to make everything all right, is it? As long as you are honest, then that excuses any behaviour, I suppose?' she jeered bitterly. 'You've told Susanna that your relationship with her won't lead to anything, so that makes it OK to sleep with her on Saturday night and send me flowers this morning? I suppose that you're going to tell me next that I'm the one in the wrong for failing to understand such a situation, for not being sophisticated enough to accept it?' Her eyes glittered for a moment with a suspicious brightness. 'But I'm glad that I'm not, because I find your attitude to relationships cold and reprehensible. Honesty is your escape clause, Brant. You tell a woman that you don't love her, then that makes it all right to walk away when you've got what you want.'

He shrugged, totally unperturbed. 'Would you find my behaviour more acceptable if I lied?' He took a sip of his whiskey before putting it carefully down beside him on the desk. 'Just forget about Susanna; she has nothing to do with us and I can assure you that you have no need to feel jealous of her,' he murmured in a tone that sounded slightly bored now.

'I'm not jealous,' Kelsey exploded, 'and there is no "us". I have already made that clear.'

'Crystal clear.' He smiled at her, and it was a strangely indulgent type of smile. 'Come here.' He held out one large hand towards her.

She stared at it suspiciously. 'What for?'

He smiled even more. 'Just come a little closer and I'll tell you. What's the matter, are you frightened?'

Frightened was probably putting it a bit strongly, but she was apprehensive about going any closer. There was something about being near to Brant that made every nerve in her body extra-sensitive. However, as she would never in a million years want him to know what effect he had on her, she did take a tentative step closer.

He caught her hand in his but made no attempt to

draw her any nearer, just stroked the smooth soft skin of her hand with one thumb in a light caress that sent ripples of awareness racing through her. 'From the first moment when we met in Joe's office there has been this magnetic attraction between us. Every time I look at you, every time I even hear your name, I can sense it. It's like a mine-field that lies between us, and neither of us has ever dared to cross it. I don't know, maybe we have both been a little too wary of the explosion we could create. . .hmm?' Unexpectedly he raised her hand to his lips and gently kissed her upturned palm. 'I'm not as cold as you like to think, Kelsey. Maybe you are right about the way I use honesty. I do find it easier to walk away from a woman when I have made it clear from the start that my intentions are not serious.' He trailed his lips in a feather-light caress to her slim wrist and the pulse that was beating wildly there. 'There would be no escape clause for you and me, Kelsey, and somehow I don't think either of us would ever want one.' He released her hand, and for a moment there was silence as Kelsey tried to gather her scattered wits together.

'You mean that once you've got your precious shares in the business that you would be willing to put up with a woman who you didn't want?' Kelsey murmured in a low tone.

'There would have to be something wrong with a man who didn't want you, Kelsey.' His eyes moved from the pallor of her face down over the gentle curves of her body in a way that gave a blatantly sexual connotation to his words.

Fiery heat licked its way through her veins, and it wasn't all entirely due to anger. There was a strange kind of excitement building up inside her tense body. Brant found her desirable! He had felt an instant attraction from the first moment he saw her! Then why had he never asked her out? a little voice asked suddenly. Why had he always treated her with such disdain?

Abruptly she turned away from him. It was all a ploy

to break down her defences—she would have to be a fool not to realise that. 'I don't understand you,' she murmured brokenly. 'I know McConell Real Estate is a very lucrative business, but you don't really need it. You have so many business interests in this town; why go to these lengths to get control of another one?'

'Because I want it, and when I make up my mind that I want something I usually get it,' he replied in a hard tone. 'I want McConell Real Estate and I want you.'

'Because I happen to come along with the business package?' she enquired, with more than a touch of bitterness in her tone.

'Partly.' She could hear a smile in his voice now. 'But also because, as I said before, you are a desirable woman.'

'This whole thing is crazy!' she exclaimed in a voice that was not exactly steady. 'A relationship between us could never work, we hardly know each other——'

'Well, that's easily remedied,' Brant cut in smoothly. 'Why don't you come home with me this evening? We can have dinner——'

'No, definitely not,' she cut in heatedly.

'Why? Have you got a date with Daniel?' He lifted his glass and finished his drink with one long swallow.

'No, I——'

'Good.' His tone was more than a little determined as he pressed the intercom on his desk. 'Betty, will you run down to Miss McConell's office and collect her bag and coat, please?'

Kelsey's anger started to rise again at this high-handed attitude and she whirled around to face him. 'Brant, I've told you——'

'Please, Kelsey.' Those words took her completely by surprise and she stared at him in astonishment, wondering if she had misheard. Had the powerfully arrogant Brant Harcourt just said please?

He grinned, a lop-sided grin that was totally disarming. 'I'd really like to spend the evening with you, Kelsey. I promise to behave like a perfect gentleman.'

'Do you know how a perfect gentleman behaves?' she asked, with an edge of dry humour in her voice.

He laughed at that. 'I'm sure you'll soon set me right if I make any slips.'

Kelsey wasn't quite so sure of any such thing as she watched the glimmer of amusement on that darkly handsome face. Just at this precise moment if he had asked her to fly to the moon and back she would have agreed. It was frightening how he only had to utter a few well-chosen words and then smile at her like that and she would agree to anything. Common sense and pride were very flimsy barriers against a man who was so powerfully attractive that he could melt you with just a look.

As Brant's white Rolls-Royce pulled to a standstill outside his huge rambling mansion of a house, Kelsey marvelled again at the ease with which he had persuaded her to come here. It was a mistake, she'd known it as soon as they had left the Harcourt McConell building, followed by a lot of curious eyes. She was treading a very dangerous path. If she had any sense she would be keeping her distance from Brant before the whole situation got out of hand.

'I suppose you know that everyone is gossiping about us at work?' she said as they stepped out of the car into the crisp autumn air. 'They probably think that we are having an affair.'

'By "they" I suppose that you mean Daniel Marsden?' Brant asked drily as he led the way up towards the front door. 'I wouldn't worry about him too much. He has so many affairs going that I doubt whether he has noticed anything yet.'

A glimmer of annoyance lit Kelsey's green eyes. Not directed towards Daniel, because she didn't really care that he saw other women, but at Brant for being so quick to point it out. Was he trying to disillusion her over

Daniel so that she would run in his direction for consolation? She wouldn't put anything past Brant. 'To quote a sentence that you seem very fond of, Brant, Daniel and I know "exactly where we stand" with each other.'

'I hope you do, Kelsey. I wouldn't like to think that you were serious about that guy.' Brant's tone was grim as he closed the door behind them with a slam.

'Why, because you are concerned about me, or because you don't want anything standing in the way of you and the McConell shares?' she asked acidly.

'A bit of both, I suppose,' he answered candidly. 'If you say no to my proposal because of Daniel, then you will be making a big mistake. Marsden likes to play the field, he's that type of guy. He certainly isn't after any heavy commitment.'

'And you would know, of course, being out of the same mould yourself,' Kelsey returned bitterly.

He shook his head. 'And that's where you are wrong, Kelsey. I am nothing at all like Marsden. My reasons for avoiding commitment since my wife's death are totally different from Marsden's.'

Kelsey would have liked very much to ask him about those reasons, but he gave her no opportunity; he was already turning away from her to lead the way through the large hall.

Kelsey had only been to Brant's house on a few occasions, but she had always admired his taste. Obviously money was no object and it had been lavished tastefully to create an elegantly sumptuous home. He had a definite eye for the good things in life, she thought now, as he led her through into what could only be described as a dream kitchen.

'Isn't Mrs Wright here today?' she asked now, as she watched Brant efficiently opening and closing the dark wood doors of the numerous kitchen cabinets.

'Even housekeepers get time off occasionally.' he smiled. 'I usually let her finish early unless I'm having a dinner party. I quite enjoy cooking, I find it very relaxing.'

'You mean that we're here on our own?' Kelsey didn't mean to sound so worried about the fact, but the words came out with a definite ring of panic.

His eyebrows rose mockingly. 'What better way for us to get to know one another?' He grinned at the look of consternation on her face. 'Don't look so worried, I don't want to test your performance in the bedroom—the kitchen, maybe.'

Her skin filled with hot embarrassed colour at this, and she had opened her mouth to make a scathing reply when he tossed an apron directly at her.

'Don't be so prudish, Kelsey, I'm only teasing. I find it very easy to wind you up, do you know that? And for some reason I do seem to enjoy doing it.' He took the jacket of his suit off and hung it over the back of one of the kitchen chairs before loosening his tie with impatient fingers. 'Maybe I like the way I can so easily bring colour into that cool porcelain skin. It makes me wonder what effect I would get if I took you into my arms and started to unbutton those strait-laced clothes you usually wear at the office.'

She was mortified to feel her colour deepening—she probably looked a lovely shade of beetroot by now—and her heart was starting to pump out some very peculiar rhythms. 'I don't wear strait-laced clothes, and for your information what you would get would be a slap across the face!' she told him succinctly.

He laughed at that. 'Well then, maybe I should warn you that retribution would follow very swiftly.'

'Somehow that doesn't surprise me,' she answered drily. 'You know, in a lot of ways you remind me of my grandfather. He always liked to have the last word on a subject, the upper hand. He was as tough as old boots.'

'Except where you were concerned.' Brant grinned over at her.

'You must be joking! He was tougher on me than he

was on anyone else. I sometimes used to wonder if he had put my father through as many hoops as he put me, or whether he was twice as hard on me because I was a female and he wanted me to prove myself.'

'So you weren't the pampered darling who could do no wrong?' There was a strange edge to his voice that made her frown.

'No, I wasn't; in fact sometimes I thought that I couldn't do anything right.' She met his eyes steadily for a moment. 'You don't have a very high opinion of me, Brant, do you?'

There was the briefest of pauses before he answered, in a light-hearted manner, 'Are you by any chance fishing for compliments, Miss McConell?'

'Certainly not!' She bent her head while she tied the apron he had tossed at her around her small waist, glad of the excuse to hide the disappointment in her face from him. She wished that he had answered that question truthfully. The fact that he had evaded it left an unpleasant lingering suspicion that his assessment of her character would be no glowing reference. 'So what help would you like me to give with dinner?' She forced a bright smile into place as she glanced back up.

'I thought I would impress you with the fact that I'm a very modern man, and an absolute genius in the kitchen, by cooking it completely unaided.' He grinned at her. 'And just to squash any rumours you might have heard about me being a chauvinist I'll allow you to uncork the wine.'

To Kelsey's surprise the evening just seemed to fly by after that. Brant hadn't been joking when he had said that he was a good cook. He prepared a delicious meal with the same efficient ease he seemed to apply to most things in life. But he seemed different, somehow, from the man he was at the office; he was more approachable, and much more relaxed. Conversation flowed easily between them as they ate dinner. They talked mostly about work and the discussion was light-hearted, never touching on anything emotive—whether Brant deliberately steered it in this direction she didn't notice. All she knew was that at some point in the evening she started to forget that this was the man she had vowed to keep her distance from.

Later, as they relaxed in the lounge over coffee and cognac, Kelsey studied her host with new eyes. He was stretched out comfortably in an armchair opposite to her. The flickering light from the log fire beside them played over his handsome features, softening the hard arrogant look that often made him seem so distant and intimidating. She had seen a new side of Brant this evening and it was a side that she liked very, very much.

'Penny for them?' he asked suddenly, catching her intent gaze.

She lowered her eyes towards the brandy glass that she was cradling in her hands. 'I was just thinking how different you seem this evening,' she admitted in a low tone.

'Different in what way?' He sounded amused now.

She shrugged, feeling slightly foolish. 'Not as hard. . . More human, I suppose.'

He laughed at that, the deep velvet tone sending a chord of shivery delight shooting through her. She loved the way he laughed like that—it made her toes curl.

'I am human, Kelsey,' he assured her now in a dulcet voice. 'And I would prove to you just how human I am, only I did promise to behave like a perfect gentleman.'

It wasn't so much his words as the dark gleam in his eyes as they raked over her slender body that made the colour start to seep up under her skin.

Desperately she searched about in her mind for something to say, some way of steering the conversation back to safe ground. 'Have. . .have I told you how much I like your house?'

He smiled at the awkward attempt. 'I believe that you have, yes.'

She moved her eyes away from his and started to relax

again as they flickered over the exquisite antique furnishings. 'You have very good taste.'

'Actually, Francesca chose a lot of the stuff in here.' There was a subtle change in his voice now, and it brought Kelsey's eyes winging back.

'I didn't realise that you lived here with your wife.' For some reason her heart had started to pound painfully in her chest. 'I thought you bought it after her death.'

He shook his head. 'We were married for three years; two of them were spent here.' His voice was flat, devoid of any emotion. 'She died just after our third anniversary, in a car crash.'

'Yes.' Kelsey inclined her head. She had read about the accident at the time; it had been in most of the papers. Francesca Harcourt had been something of a celebrity in the city, for not only had she been a successful model, she had also come from a very eminent family. 'It was a terrible tragedy,' she murmured gently. 'You must have been devastated.'

He didn't answer her immediately; shadows cast by the firelight played across the strong face, highlighting a look of utter bleakness for just a second. In that moment Kelsey's heart filled with compassion for him. How awful to lose your wife after only a few short years together. She remembered her own grief after her parents' death, and she longed to be able to go across to him and put her arms around him. He glanced up and their eyes met.

'You still haven't got over her death, have you?' Kelsey whispered.

'There are some things in life that you never get over, Kelsey, you just learn to live with them.' He stretched out a hand and switched on a table-lamp beside him. Bright golden light dispelled the shadows and once again Brant's features were coolly composed as he glanced at his wristwatch. 'It's nearly midnight, time I got you home.'

They drove back towards town in silence. Glancing at

Brant, she felt sure that his thoughts were still in the past, still with Francesca, and her heart squeezed painfully.

'Thank you for a lovely evening.' She was the first to speak as his car pulled up outside her apartment.

He put on the hand-brake, but didn't switch off the engine. 'I'm glad you enjoyed it.' He half turned in his seat. 'Maybe we can do it again some time?'

She hesitated for only a second before nodding. She wanted to spend time with him. The need to be with him, to get close to him, was so strong that it was like an actual pain inside.

He smiled. 'I believe there is a good play on at the O'Keefe centre. 'Would you like to go, say, Wednesday night?'

She pretended to give it some thought before saying lightly, 'Yes, that would be lovely.'

He looked pleased, and Kelsey tried to persuade herself that he was glad that she had accepted because he had enjoyed her company, because he liked her, and for no other more devious reason.

He leaned across towards her and her heart leapt wildly as she wondered if he was going to kiss her, but he was merely opening the door for her.

'Goodnight, then.' She gave him a small smile.

'Goodnight, Kelsey.' Dark eyes lingered on the paleness of her skin and the soft fullness of her lips before she turned away and climbed gracefully out of the car.

He waited until she had reached the door of her apartment and had opened it before driving away. For a moment she stood and watched until the tail-lights of the Rolls had disappeared into the darkness of the night, and for the first time she allowed herself to think seriously about the possibility of marrying Brant Harcourt.

CHAPTER FIVE

KELSEY stared down at the documents on her desk. It was Monday morning, exactly two weeks since Brant had taken her to his house for dinner. Two weeks that had been filled with trips to the theatre, lunches, dinners. One invitation had followed another so smoothly, so naturally that Kelsey had no problem in just allowing herself to be swept along by it all.

The words on the sheet of paper danced in front of her eyes as she thought about their date last night. Brant had taken her to the same restaurant where he had proposed marriage the day her grandfather's will had been read. She had felt sure when he had suggested that particular restaurant that he was going to ask her again. She had even decided on the answer that she would give. She was going to say yes.

She hadn't fooled herself into thinking that Brant was in love with her. She was enough of a realist to know that he was not, that much had not changed. What *had* changed was their perception of each other. Brant's manner towards her had become much more gentle and relaxed, as if he genuinely had started to enjoy her company. Kelsey felt as if she was getting to know the real Brant, the man who was hidden behind that hard businesslike exterior, and the more she got to know him the deeper her feelings for him were growing. She thought she understood a little better what made him so tough, so unapproachable at times. The death of his wife had obviously affected him deeply—it was probably what made him so cynical about love and relationships. Kelsey was starting to hope that maybe she would be the one to change all that. That maybe one day he would feel the same way about her as she did about him. Until then, perhaps she had enough love for both of them.

These were the thoughts that had whirled through her mind as they had dined last night. They had lingered for a long time over coffee and liqueurs. Candlelight had flickered, the mood had been relaxed, yet intimate, when Brant had leaned closer to tell her in a low voice that he had something for her.

She had immediately thought that it would be an engagement ring and she had swallowed down a rush of nervous excitement.

The box that he had taken from his jacket pocket was a long grey velvet one with a designer's name stamped in gold on the outside. Her heart had fallen a little as she had realised it wasn't a ring. She had given him an uncertain smile, and opened the box with fingers that were not completely steady.

The subdued lighting of the restaurant had caught and played over the brilliant blaze of emeralds and diamonds in the necklace within. Her breath had caught in a gasp. 'It. . .it's beautiful, Brant.' She glanced over at the cool dark face that was watching her so intently. 'I. . . I don't know what to say.'

'Then don't say anything,' he smiled. 'There are times when you have no need of words, Kelsey. Those express-ive eyes of yours speak very clearly for you.'

This piece of information disconcerted her for a moment. What else had he read in her eyes? Did he guess the true extent of her feelings for him? Her pride rebelled for just a moment against such a thought before she pushed it to one side. She loved this man and she wanted to marry him—pride would have to take a back seat for a while to those feelings. Besides, if she let him know how much she cared about him, how much she loved him, maybe it would be all to the good. Love was a two-way thing, if you gave it you stood a better chance of receiving it back.

She was about to take the necklace from the box, when he stopped her. 'I'll put that on for you later.'

She glanced across at him. The dark face was impassive, yet there was a gleam in the dark eyes that sent a shiver of desire flowing through her. She closed the jewellery case with a snap.

Later, when he pulled the car up outside her apartment, she invited him inside for the first time.

'No, I won't come in, Kelsey. I've got a devil of a court case on tomorrow and I still have some work to do on it tonight.'

She was surprised by his refusal, and a little hurt. She had allowed herself to hope that maybe tonight he was going to take her into his arms and kiss her. . .really kiss her, not just that tormentingly light brush of his lips that sealed the end of most of their evenings out.

'But first let me see this on you.' He took the jewellery-box from his jacket and opened it.

Emeralds and diamonds glittered softly in the moonlight as he unfastened the clasp with decisive fingers and reached towards her.

She lifted her honey-gold hair from her shoulders as he fastened the chain around her neck. She could smell the lovely elusive aroma that always surrounded him. It gave her a strange sensation in the pit of her stomach, like being pushed too hard and too high on a swing.

He sat back and she released her hair, letting it tumble around her shoulders in shining waves. For a moment they just stared at each other. His face was in shadow, so she couldn't tell what he was thinking. She was swathed in the silvery light from outside; it caught the cool gleam of gold in her hair and played with haunting beauty over the brilliant gemstones at her throat. Her skin was creamy white, her eyes as bright as the emeralds she wore.

He muttered something under his breath and then he was leaning forward. She closed her eyes, waiting for the light exquisite pleasure of his lips against hers. Instead his lips touched the side of her neck, gently at first, and then more heatedly. A delicious shiver ran through her and she lifted her hands to burrow her fingers into the thick darkness of his hair.

His lips trailed over the sensitive area at the side of her neck. His hands moved from her waist up to her breasts, rested there lightly for a moment, before shaping their soft curves through the white silky material of her dress. He caressed her gently, then the touch of his fingers grew stronger, more intense. A small moan of ecstasy escaped her lips before he covered them with his.

His kiss was slow, drugging and very sensual. Kelsey's body had never felt as alive as it did at that moment; all her senses seemed to have flown into wild and chaotic disarray. Her heart was pounding so heavily that she felt sure he could feel it against the hand that moved in a skilled and knowing way over the fullness of her breast. The touch of his hand, the pressure of his mouth drove her out of her mind with the need to be closer to him.

He lifted his head slowly, and her fingers tightened in his hair.

'Don't stop.' Was that husky-sounding voice really hers? She could sense the smile hovering on his lips rather than see it. Then he lowered his head and took possession of her lips once again. This time, however, it was only a brief hard kiss and his hand left the warm curve of her breasts, leaving them heavy and aching with raw desire.

'Brant?' She looked up at him pleadingly as he pulled away. 'I don't want you to stop. I want you to make love to me.' Her voice was softly slurred with need and she hardly recognised it as her own.

The strong mouth curved in a half-smile. 'And I want to make love to you.' His eyes moved down over the jewels at her creamy throat to the firm thrust of her breasts in the white silk dress. 'Very much,' he added softly. 'But not now. It isn't the right time.'

She frowned and stared up at him uncomprehendingly. She had lowered her every barrier, had lost every scrap of pride as she practically begged him to make love to her; and he had refused! She couldn't understand him; a moment ago his kisses had burnt, they had been so hot, and now he was coldly telling her that it wasn't the right time! She felt humiliated, bewildered.

'Don't look at me like that, Kelsey.' He gently reached out a hand and tipped her chin further upwards.

'Like what?' She pulled away from him, and he smiled.

'Run along inside now,' he said gently. 'We'll talk tomorrow.'

She stared at him. A few moments ago he had been treating her like a woman, now. . .now he was treating her as if she were a little girl.

She turned towards the car door. 'Kelsey.' His voice halted her briefly. 'Soon, very soon, we will make love.'

That promise rang in her ears now at her office desk, as she stared down at the work in front of her. One moment she felt anger towards Brant, the next anger at herself for losing control so easily. When the anger faded other emotions flowed in to plague her. She had never felt so vulnerable, so unsure of herself in her life before.

There was a light tap at the door, and Daniel Marsden walked in.

'Well, hello, stranger.' He grinned at her. 'Thought I'd come and visit for a moment as I don't get to see much of you these days. What have you been doing with yourself?'

'Not much, really,' she murmured vaguely, feeling a little uncomfortable as she wondered if he knew about her dates with Brant.

'Now, don't be evasive with me, Kel.' He crossed towards her and perched on the edge of her desk. 'A little birdie told me that you've been playing footsie with the boss.'

'No, I. . .' She glanced up, and, catching the gleam of

amusement on his face, she relaxed. He wasn't annoyed with her, just teasing. 'Well, I have been seeing him,' she admitted softly, two bright spots of colour burning on her cheeks.

'I knew it.' He shook his head. 'In fact I knew it the night I took you to George's party and you tried to tell me you didn't much care for the guy. When I saw the way you danced with him I knew I'd lost my dinner companion for a while.'

Kelsey didn't know if she cared much for that last comment. What did he mean by 'for a while'? Was that his way of warning her that this would not last for long, or was he merely being funny? Glancing at those handsome features, it was hard to tell. He looked as if he was joking.

'Actually, Kel, there was something that I wanted to discuss with you if you are free for lunch?' He was suddenly serious now.

'Oh?' She frowned, intrigued by this. 'What is it? Something to do with work?'

'No.' He grinned, back to his old teasing self. 'You'll have to have lunch with me to find out.'

'Well. . .' She hesitated, unsure. She had lunch with Brant most days now.

'Brant's at court today, Kel; he won't be back until much later. It's the Daubaussey trial today.' He correctly guessed the reason for her uncertainty.

'Oh, well, in that case yes, I would love to have lunch with you.' She fought down the flood of embarrassed colour that threatened to light her face, and he grinned.

'Does about one suit you?'

'I think so. Check with Maggie on the way out, will you?'

'Right you are.' With another grin he left her to once more struggle with the work on her desk.

It was something of a relief to leave it at lunchtime when Daniel came back into the office. Although she was trying very hard not to let her private life intrude into her work, she felt she was fighting a losing battle these days.

'We'll be around the corner at the Mint,' she told her secretary on the way out of the door, and got an oddly disapproving look.

'I wonder what's the matter with Maggie?' she murmured to Daniel, as they waited for the elevator.

'Maybe she thinks that you are two-timing the boss.' He grinned. 'Maybe we should have sneaked out of here separately, I'd hate to see Brant in a jealous rage.'

The idea was so ludicrous that Kelsey threw her head back and laughed. 'I doubt that Brant has ever experienced a jealous thought, let alone a rage, in his entire life.' Especially where I'm concerned, she thought to herself, and the laughter died on her lips.

The Mint was terribly crowded, as it always was at lunchtime. They had to wait for a table and, when they got one, it was right in the middle of the room and not very private.

Daniel grimaced. 'Perhaps we should have gone somewhere else.'

'No, this is fine,' she assured him with a smile. 'Besides, we don't really have much time for going somewhere else.'

He nodded, and his eyes lingered on her face for a moment, taking in the sparkle in her wide-spaced green eyes, the delicate colour in her high cheekbones. 'Love is agreeing with you, Kel; you look radiant.'

His words made her colour deepen. 'Who said anything about love?' she jested lightly.

'You don't need to say it, I have eyes in my head. I just hope Brant appreciates what he's got,' he said with a wry twist of his lips. 'You know, Kelsey, I have missed our dinner dates. I've always enjoyed your company and felt relaxed around you.' He reached across impulsively and covered her slender hands with his. 'I hope we will always remain friends, Kel. I know that you're serious about Brant and that you're not going to be able to see me as much now, if at all. But I just want you to know that I'm here for you if you ever need a friend to talk to.'

Kelsey was surprised by the sincerity in his voice, and a little overwhelmed by it. 'Thank you, Daniel,' she murmured softly. 'I will always value our friendship.' As she moved her hand gently away from his her eyes caught and held with a pair of hostile blue ones on the next table. Susanna Winters was watching her intently, a look of utter dislike on her beautiful face, before she turned her attention back to the man whom she was sitting with.

'Anyway, enough of all this sentiment,' Daniel berated himself. 'Actually, I really wanted to talk about something else.'

'Oh?' Kelsey returned her attention to him.

'I've heard a little rumour that you are thinking of selling your grandfather's house.'

Kelsey's eyebrows rose in surprise. 'Yes, I am.'

'Well, I'm very interested in buying it, very interested indeed,' he told her earnestly.

'You are? What about your bachelor-pad in town? I would have thought that was much more your style than an old rambling house that is quite a distance out.'

'Well, I shall keep the pad,' he smiled. 'Just for sentimental reasons, of course.'

'Of course.' She thought about his apartment and grinned. It was blatantly a place for seduction. She had only visited it once, and she remembered feeling very uncomfortable. Not that Daniel had made any move on her—well, no more than the usual few kisses—but the blatant sensuality of the décor had put her very much on her guard. She recalled the water-bed with the black silk sheets that she had glimpsed through an open door, and wondered again why he would be interested in her grandfather's old house, it was definitely not his kind of place.

'I would like to make you an offer for it, Kelsey,' he said now.

'Perhaps you should come out and take a look at it again first,' she suggested.

He nodded his head. 'I'd like that very much. When would suit you? I'm free tonight if that's all right?'

'Well, I don't know.' She frowned, wondering if Brant would want to see her this evening.

'I'll tell you what, you check with him and get back to me.' Once again Daniel guessed the reason for her hesitation.

She smiled. 'Am I so easy to read?'

'Transparent,' came the disconcerting reply. 'You've got it bad, Kelsey, real bad. I just hope it works out for you.' The note of doubt in his voice did nothing for her confidence on that score.

They were late getting back to the office, but Kelsey did feel a little more relaxed than when she had gone out. She didn't think it would take her too long to catch up with work now, and if she wasn't on schedule by the end of the day she would stay late and get it done.

Maggie looked a trifle irate as she came in. 'Mr Harcourt has been looking for you,' she muttered, a note of censure in her voice. 'He asked if you would go straight up to his office when you came in.'

Kelsey nodded and turned back towards the elevators. She didn't feel as intimidated as she'd used to when summoned up here, but there was a certain feeling of apprehension, her nerves still tingled as she turned the handle and walked into his secretary's office.

Susanna Winters was on her way out from seeing Brant. Kelsey nodded her head in acknowledgement as they passed, and received a look that could only be described as calculating in return.

'You can go right in, Miss McConell,' Brant's secretary informed her.

'Thank you.'

Brant was sitting at his desk, immersed in some documents that were spread out before him. These days he usually stood when she came in, and left what he was doing to give her a brief kiss on the cheek. Today he merely glanced up. 'I won't be a moment, take a seat,' he murmured absently, as if she were a client.

Kelsey sat down in the leather-upholstered chair opposite him and studied the top of his dark head. Was this cool stranger the man who had kissed her so passionately last night? How had she ever had the nerve—the audacity to ask him to make love to her? She squirmed slightly in the chair and two bright orbs of colour lit her features.

He glanced up, his eyes swiftly raked over her slim figure in the Prince of Wales check suit and then lingered on her face, noting her heightened colour. His eyes were cold and hard; there was no flicker of emotion.

She swallowed nervously. 'Did you win the Daubaussey case?' she asked, at a loss for anything else to say to cover her embarrassment.

'Yes, I did.' His voice was matter-of-fact, almost offhand. 'I wrapped it up earlier than I thought and called into your office to ask if you would like to have lunch with me.'

'Oh. . .sorry. I was out with Daniel——' she started to explain, but he cut across her.

'I know where you were.' His voice was so frosty that she was taken aback. Was he a tiny bit jealous? she wondered suddenly. Her heart started to lift. If he was, then maybe he was starting to care about her, maybe she was starting to reach through those steel-like barriers.

'It wasn't anything, really. He just wanted to talk to me about——'

'I don't want to know what you talked about, Kelsey; that is your business.' He interrupted her explanations ruthlessly, killing any hope that she had that he might be in any way jealous. 'What is my concern is the fact that you are. . .' he glanced at his gold wrist-watch,

'. . .exactly three quarters of an hour late back from lunch.'

Her eyes widened; he had called her up here to reprimand her for being late! She could hardly believe her ears.

'Well, I'm——'

'It's not good enough, Kelsey,' he interrupted her again. 'You are way behind with the Fitzroy case. I wanted that finished by the end of the week. What the hell's the matter with you, anyway?' he grated harshly.

She stared at him, at the hard rugged features, the firm mouth that was capable of stirring up so much emotion in her. You are the problem, she wanted to scream at him. You are in my mind all the time. Thoughts of you, of our relationship, are plaguing me night and day. She remained silent, an unconsciously militant light in her beautiful eyes.

'I'm sorry, Brant.' Her voice held quiet dignity. 'You are not usually so rigid about time, but I can assure you that it won't happen again.' It was a slight dig at the fact that they had been late back from lunch a few times these last few weeks. Whether it reached its mark she wasn't sure. There was no change of expression on the harsh features. 'As for the Fitzroy case, I know I'm behind, but it will all be completed on schedule.'

'I'm glad to hear it. I did warn you once before that you would get no special favours from me, Kelsey. No matter what the circumstances, if your work is not up to standard then you will have to face the consequences.' The cold voice was unequivocal.

'And I think I told you that I have never asked for special favours, nor do I want any,' she answered stiffly, her hands curled into tight fists on her lap. 'Was there anything else?' She slid forward in her chair, anxious to leave before her cool poise deserted her.

'Yes.' For a fraction of a second his gaze lingered on her lips. Then he reached to open the top drawer of his desk to take out a small grey box. 'I got this for you at lunchtime.'

She stared at the box sitting on top of the pile of legal documents and a shaft of some indescribable emotion hit her heart.

He opened the lid and a beautiful emerald and diamond engagement ring flashed fire under the desk light.

'It's beautiful.' Her voice sounded as numb as she felt.

He got up from his chair and came around towards her. The dark suit was perfectly tailored to the lithe, powerful body. It made him appear taller than his six feet two inches, or perhaps that was because of the angle she had to tip her head to look up at him.

Taking her left hand firmly in his, he took the ring from the box and slid it firmly on to her finger. It fitted perfectly and it was probably the most spectacular engagement ring she had ever seen.

Her eyes misted as she looked at it, and green merged into the icy-blue lights of the diamonds. Why had he chosen this moment to give it to her? Why hadn't he produced it when the mood between them was tender? Last night, or even tomorrow, when she could try to forget the hard look on his face this afternoon? Why now, in the cold light of day, and after an even colder exchange of words?

'I want your answer, Kelsey, and I want it now,' he told her firmly.

She hesitated; part of her wanted to throw the ring back at him, the part of her that was logical, the part that held her pride and her anger. But there was another side of her that wanted to accept, because she loved him, because she wanted very much to be his wife. She knew that if she turned him down she would regret it for a long time. It might take forever to get over Brant Harcourt.

She stared up into those cool dark eyes and then she heard herself say something that took even her by surprise. 'If you make me a partner in the Real Estate business, then the answer is yes.'

There was a flicker of some emotion in the depths of those eyes. What it was she couldn't have said—surprise? Regret? 'Well, well,' he murmured smoothly. 'So there is a more materialistic young woman hiding beneath the soft feminine veneer!'

She didn't make any reply to that. Maybe it was better to let him think like that—at least it would let him know that, although he could dominate her body and her senses with his kisses, she was no walk-over. She could play him at his own game. 'And I want to go into court more. I'm tired of those dry corporate cases you keep asking me to research. I want something I can get my teeth into.'

He looked amused now. 'I hope I haven't created some power-mad monster,' he murmured drily.

'What is that supposed to mean?' she demanded sharply.

He shrugged. 'Just that when I suggested marriage for business reasons two weeks ago you were outraged. Now you are dictating terms.'

She shrugged. 'I suppose I'm starting to play this by your rules. You told me I shouldn't view marriage through a haze of emotionalism, that I should think it through coolly and be practical. I guess that's what I have done.'

He stared at her as if not sure whether she amused him or not now. 'You never cease to amaze me, do you know that, Kelsey?' he said softly.

'Good.' She gave him a strained smile. 'But I don't see why you should be so surprised by my request. Men don't hold the monopoly on being business-minded and analytical. Just because I like the way you kiss me it doesn't mean my brain has stopped functioning. I can see that marriage to you might be a good deal for me.' She swallowed hard. How on earth had she managed to say something like that? The frightening thing was that she actually sounded convincing!

He moved away from her back behind his desk. Sitting down, he regarded her contemplatively through narrowed eyes. 'You are not ready for too much court work yet. That was one of the reasons we decided not to give you the junior partnership: Joe was of the opinion that——'

'I know what Joe's opinions were on my career,' Kelsey cut across him impatiently. 'He thought that I should be married with six children, preferably boys. That my place was in a kitchen not a court of law. If you are trying to tell me that your outlook is the same, then——'

'I am not trying to tell you any such thing,' he interrupted smoothly. 'I'm all for your pursuing your career. I don't think the cosy domestic scene that Joe envisaged for you would suit our marriage anyway.'

Silence met that remark. Kelsey's heart seemed to have plunged somewhere down towards her shoes. Did that mean that Brant didn't want children? That he would prefer her to put her energies into her career rather than her home life? She moistened dry lips with the tip of her tongue. 'So what type of marriage do you envisage for us?'

He shrugged. 'Successful, I hope.' His mouth curved in a dry smile. 'Don't worry, Kelsey, I won't curtail your career plans. We will have a modern marriage; you can go your way, and I'll go mine. How does that suit you?'

It didn't, it didn't suit at all. Maybe she could live without children—and that was a big maybe—but she couldn't live with a man who had affairs with other women, and by the sound of things that was what he had in mind. If that was the case, then there was no way she could marry him. It would kill her to live with him and to love him and to know that there were other women in his life.

She hesitated and then, choosing her words very carefully, she asked the question that really mattered to her, the question that would decide whether or not she married him. 'By going your own way, do you mean that you intend to have affairs?'

He leaned back in his chair. The dark handsome features were solemn, the eyes that met hers direct and unwavering. 'No, I don't intend to have affairs. As long as you are sharing my bed I don't think there will be any need for me to have affairs.' His fingers drummed softly on the desk-top. 'You do intend to share my bed, I take it?'

He asked that question as if it were the topic for discussion at one of their business meetings. It startled Kelsey; it also embarrassed her.

'I. . .well, I. . .' She fought down the rising colour in her cheeks to little avail. 'I suppose so. . .yes.'

'Good.' The strong mouth curved into a semblance of a smile. 'Because my idea of a modern marriage is not one where we are sleeping around.'

She was relieved to hear it, so relieved that her blood was singing through her veins now, and she could almost forget his cold manner.

Her feeling of elation was brief as Brant continued tersely, 'As for your request to be made a partner, there is no way, Kelsey, that I am going to give you an equal say in the running of the McConell business. After all, the whole reason for our marriage is that I gain complete control.'

There was an over-bright glitter in Kelsey's eyes as she stared across at the harshly remote features. Did he have to be so blunt? So cruelly insensitive? She didn't need or want him to point out the reasons for their marriage. That was something she wanted to forget about. She wanted to dream her own romantic thoughts. She wanted to hope that Brant would one day realise that he was in love with her, that it was his grief over losing his wife that had blinded him to a new love. It was unrealistic and quixotic, she knew, but she needed to keep that hope alive at the back of her mind.

'I'm in charge of the business, Kelsey, and you reap the financial rewards. That is the deal,' he continued firmly.

She dropped her eyes from his. It was hard to school her features into a cool unemotional mask when she felt her heart was squeezed into a tight painful knot. Business was the most important thing in Brant's life, but it wouldn't always be, she told herself resolutely. One day she would break through the wall of ice that surrounded his heart.

She raised her chin and met his eyes with a look that was equally as determined as his. 'All right, I'll accept that. But I want you to give me a junior partnership here.'

There was silence for a moment and she felt her nerves flutter with panic, but she was glad that she had stood her ground and made the request. She wanted Brant to know that she wasn't a little mouse, that she was as much of a business person as he was. 'I am good at my job, Brant. I just need a chance to prove myself.'

He picked up a gold pen and tapped it thoughtfully against the papers in front of him. 'All right.' He sat forward suddenly and reached for his desk diary.

'All right what?' She frowned, and he looked across at her.

'All right, you can have a junior partnership,' he told her decisively. 'You're right, you are good at your job. I probably would have offered you one some time soon anyway.'

A lovely smile lit up her face. It was only a small victory but it meant such a lot to her, especially the words of praise about her work. Brant never handed out praise lightly.

'So, how does the twenty-first suit you?' Brant went on to ask calmly.

'Sorry?' She stared at him blankly.

'For our wedding,' he explained steadily. 'I think we could have all the paperwork sorted out by then, and we are within the time limit of Joe's will.'

'Oh, I see. . .' She swallowed down a lump in her throat. 'Yes, I think that will suit. I'll have to check my diary, of course.' Was that really her voice? So cool and calm. It was a million miles away from the way she wanted things to be. She wanted him to take her into his arms and kiss her. A wedding proposal should be sealed with a kiss, not with a lot of legal documents and a business discussion.

His dark face was impassive. He merely nodded.

'Right, well, if you will excuse me I'll get back to my work.' She started to get hurriedly to her feet, anxious to get away now while her mask of calm indifference was still in place.

As she moved her engagement ring caught the light and sparkled with a brilliance that was breathtaking. She hadn't thanked him for it, she realised suddenly. She had hardly said anything about it at all. She glanced at the set features across the desk and decided to leave it that way. To Brant the ring was a seal on a business deal. What was the point in meaningless words?

With her head held high she turned and left the room. She might have to wait a while for Brant's love, but in the meantime she was determined to have his respect. Maybe one thing would lead to another, a hopeful voice whispered in her heart.

CHAPTER SIX

KELSEY stood in front of the cheval-glass and studied her reflection critically. The taffeta dress was a pale colour of champagne and it reached nearly to the floor. She had had it designed and made especially for her by a leading fashion house. It had cost a fortune but she had considered it money well spent when she had first tried it on. Now she wasn't so sure.

There was no doubting that it was beautiful. Romantic, dreamy, innocent, it was all the things that a wedding dress should be. It was just that it wasn't right for her wedding to Brant. He would take one look at it and hate it, she knew he would.

She sighed; it was a little late for that observation, seeing as she was about to become Mrs Brant Harcourt in about half an hour's time. . . Nerves stirred and fluttered.

She leaned closer to her reflection and studied her make-up. She had had it done by a professional make-up artist. Her own hands had not been steady enough for the task this morning. She had to admit the girl had done a good job. The look was understated and natural, yet it gave her a radiant glow; no one looking at her would guess that she hadn't slept at all last night, that she had tossed and turned and worried herself sick.

Her hair was swept up and away from her face into a riot of curls. The style complemented the make-up. It added to the overall effect of gentle, innocent beauty. Kelsey turned angrily away from the reflection. That was it, she realised suddenly. That was the thing that was wrong. She looked too romantic, too innocent, and there was no room in Brant's high-powered, tough world for such things. He would look at her and despise her.

She crossed towards the window and stared out. The day was crisp and bright, not a cloud in the clear blue of the sky. The leaves on the trees in the little park across the road were turning glorious shades of russet and gold. Her eyes moved over the scene idly, her mind in turmoil. What would happen tonight when Brant found out that she was every bit as innocent as she looked? Her nerves twisted and pulled in all directions. She shouldn't be thinking about that, she should just let things take their course naturally. Brant might not even notice her innocence—now that was a ridiculous thought. Of course he would notice, he was an experienced man of the world.

The shrill ring of the doorbell shattered the quiet of her flat. That would be the car that Brant had said he would send. She glanced at her watch—it was early, fifteen minutes early. Her nerves stretched and screamed at her; there was no way that she was leaving here until exactly one o'clock. She crossed towards the door and opened it.

A chauffeur in dark uniform stood on the doorstep. Behind him stood a cream Rolls-Royce Phantom.

'I'm not ready yet,' she told him without preamble. 'I'll be another ten minutes at least.'

He tipped his hat. 'That's fine, Miss McConell. I just wanted you to know that I'm here.' With that he turned and walked lazily back towards the car.

Kelsey didn't really know what to do with herself when she went back inside. She was ready, had been for over an hour. She wandered aimlessly around the place. It had been stripped of all her most personal possessions. Pictures, ornaments, books, all had been neatly packed and transferred to Brant's house. They were sitting in one of his spare bedrooms now. A few tea-chests and a couple of large trunks, all her worldly possessions.

Brant hadn't consulted her as to where they should live after they were married. He had assumed that she would want to move into his house; it was the practical thing to do, after all. 'You may as well put your apartment up for sale,' he had told her in passing a few days ago, but she'd been busy, and hadn't got round to it.

She went upstairs towards her bedroom. The wardrobes were empty except for one outfit that she had worn yesterday and a little fur-trimmed jacket that had been made to fit over her wedding dress. She sat down on her bed and glanced at her alarm clock on the table beside her. Almost ten to one; in approximately half an hour she would be a married woman. Next to the clock there was a women's magazine. She had bought it last week because they had written an article about her forthcoming wedding. She picked it up now and it fell open at the appropriate page, proof of how much she had looked at it these last few days.

They had rung her and asked if they could interview her a couple of weeks ago. She had refused. She had known the type of story they would want her to give them. How the city's most powerful and affluent lawyer had fallen head over heels in love with her. She wasn't that good at lying; her refusal had been abrupt.

They ran the story from a different angle, based it more on Brant's previous marriage than on his forthcoming one. There was a picture of Kelsey as she left the Harcourt offices. It was an awful shot. She was wearing a plain grey suit, her hair was scraped back from her face, and she looked pale and tired. The photographer had caught her unawares; her thoughts had been far away on Brant and how distant he seemed. Since they had set the date for their wedding he had treated her like a stranger. He was always polite, she couldn't complain about his manners, but he was always cool with her and very formal.

Inset they had printed a photograph of Brant with his arm around Francesca. It had been taken at a charity ball about a year before her death. They were both smiling, and they looked very happy. Francesca was exquisitely beautiful. Her long blonde hair was a lighter shade than Kelsey's, her figure that of a model, very slim. She had the type of body that would have looked good dressed in a sack. The little black beaded dress she was wearing in the photograph looked sensational.

Underneath the photograph they had printed the words 'Very much in love'. Kelsey stared at it, a curious aching feeling behind her eyes. She hated the article, she hated the way they had titled it 'THE NEXT MRS HAR-COURT'. It made her feel second best and inadequate. Her eyes moved down over the printed page. There was a piece at the bottom which quoted a source, who was reportedly close to both her and Brant, as saying, 'The marriage was a shrewd move and very good news for the Harcourt McConell business.'

Who on earth had said that? she wondered again. Somebody at the offices, probably. The news of her marriage to Brant had caused quite a sensation at work. She closed the magazine with a snap. She shouldn't be reading it, especially now, a few moments before she was due to leave for her wedding. If Brant had loved her she would have said it was trash, drivel—she wouldn't even have picked it up.

The doorbell rang and the magazine slid to the floor. It was time for her to leave. Was she doing the right thing? The question raced through her mind and didn't seem to want to leave it. She picked up her jacket from the wardrobe and made her way slowly downstairs.

She thought about all the people who would be there to watch her wedding. It was only supposed to be a quiet civil ceremony, none of the fuss that was associated with a church wedding, yet the number of people who were to attend it had risen dramatically from the handful they had decided on. They were mostly colleagues from work who had just expected to be asked, and then there was Brant's mother who had flown in this morning from England. Kelsey clenched her hands into tight fists at her side; she was not going to be able to go through with this, she thought suddenly. She had allowed herself to hope that Brant might one day come to love her, that she stood a strong chance of making their marriage a success. Now her confidence seemed to have deserted her and that hope seemed foolish and improbable.

The doorbell rang again and she moved across to answer it, ready to tell the chauffeur that she would not be leaving with him, that there would be no wedding.

However, it wasn't the chauffeur that stood on the step, but a delivery man. 'Miss McConell?' he enquired briskly.

She nodded, and he handed her a single red rose.

Her heart lifted and sang. There was no card attached to the flower, but in the language of flowers a red rose symbolised true love—didn't it?

'Miss McConell, if we don't leave now you are going to be late.' The chauffeur moved around the car towards her, a worried frown on his face.

'Yes, I know.' She stared at the deep red petals of the rose, petals that had not fully opened yet. 'I'm ready now,' she told him softly.

A large crowd was waiting for her as the car pulled in at its destination. A sea of faces turned to watch her as the chauffeur came around to open the door of the Rolls, and she climbed out gracefully. The only person she saw was Brant.

He looked overpoweringly handsome. A dark suit that sat so easily on those broad shoulders, a grey silk cravat at the strong neck, a white carnation in his lapel. He detached himself from the crowd and moved towards her.

'I was just starting to wonder if you were going to stand me up!' One dark eyebrow rose quizzically, then his eyes moved leisurely over the soft radiance of her complexion, the deep emerald-green eyes that were alive with vivid sparkling light, the delicately curving figure in the champagne taffeta. 'You were certainly worth waiting for,' he murmured softly. There was a note in his voice that puzzled her slightly; she searched his face anxiously, fearful that she would find sarcasm behind his words. There was none; the arrogantly handsome features held a warmth and sincerity that made her heart melt with sheer joy. She smiled up at him and he took her hand to lead her inside where their life together would begin.

It was over so quickly. One moment she was Kelsey McConell, the next, Mrs Brant Harcourt. It was all like a dream; Kelsey felt slightly dazed as they stepped back out into the glorious sunshine surrounded by people who wanted to congratulate them. Somebody threw confetti; it caught in Kelsey's blonde curls and in the folds of the taffeta dress, and it missed Brant completely. Photographs were taken. Brant's mother stepped forward and kissed them both. There were tears in her eyes, Kelsey noticed, and her heart immediately went out to her, even though they had never met before, had never spoken.

Brant put his arm around Kelsey's waist as he spoke to the crowd. 'We hope to see you all back at the hotel for a champagne reception.'

'You haven't kissed the bride yet!' somebody called.

Brant grinned ruefully, and then, catching Kelsey unawares, he swung her across him in a dramatic embrace. He looked down at her and in that moment before his lips came down to hers there was an expression in them that was almost like regret. Then his lips met hers and she felt sure she had imagined it, for that kiss was sensational.

When Brant released her everyone was cheering and clapping. He smiled. 'Show's over, folks. Let's get to that hotel otherwise Kelsey and I just might miss our flight this evening.'

Kelsey laughed up at him as they climbed back into the Rolls-Royce Phantom. 'Are you going to tell me where you are taking me on that flight this evening?'

'Certainly not.' He grinned at her. 'Our honeymoon is a closely guarded secret. That way I'm certain we will have no interruptions.'

Kelsey swallowed down a sudden stirring of nerves at the thought of them alone together.

'Do you know they actually phoned me this morning from the office and I had to go in and sort out the details of the Shaunessey case for next week? I swear if they knew where we were honeymooning they would want to come along.'

Some more than others, Kelsey couldn't help thinking as she recalled seeing Susanna Winters's face among the crowd a little while ago.

The reception was held at Chequers Hall, a large rambling hotel that stood on the bank of Lake Ontario. The hotel had set out a fabulous buffet in the largest of the function-rooms. The soft clink of crystal glasses and the gentle murmur of conversation blended as Brant and Kelsey mingled with their guests.

At some point they were separated. Brant was detained by a group of business associates who wanted to discuss a controversial court case he had handled successfully last year.

Helen Harcourt, spying her daughter-in-law momentarily alone, moved quickly across to her.

'Well, my dear, can I say how beautiful you look? Truly a radiant bride.' The perfectly modulated English accent was very attractive.

'Thank you.' Kelsey smiled shyly at the older woman, thinking how elegant she looked in the pale blue silk suit and how much Brant resembled his mother; the same dark hair and eyes.

'Brant's really very secretive, you know,' Helen continued. 'He had never even hinted to me that he was seeing someone seriously. It was a quite a shock when he rang me a couple of days ago to tell me he was getting married again. He doesn't believe in giving me much warning. It was the same last time, a real whirlwind romance.'

A flicker of emotion crossed Kelsey's face at this. She

didn't know anything about Brant's courtship with Francesca, and somehow she didn't think she wanted to know.

Helen's sharp eye noted the change of expression and she leaned across to take Kelsey's hand. 'I'm sorry, my dear. I've been indelicate, talking of things in the past like that.'

'No. . .no, it's quite all right.' Kelsey hastily tried to reassure the woman that she didn't mind a bit.

Helen patted her hand. 'You're a warm-hearted, sensitive woman, Kelsey. I couldn't have wished for a lovelier daughter-in-law. And Brant adores you; the love on his face when he saw you stepping out of that car brought a tear to my eye.'

To Kelsey's consternation her own eyes filled with tears at this. 'Did he really look at me like that?' Her voice shook a little with emotion, she wanted so much to believe what Helen was saying.

'Of course.' Dark intelligent eyes lingered on the delicate flush that lit Kelsey's porcelain skin. 'You are just what he has needed, Kelsey,' she said softly.

Does he need me, Kelsey wondered suddenly, really need me? Her tears threatened to brim over now. For some reason her emotions felt as if they were on a see-saw, sliding up and down, dizzying heights, frightening lows.

'Well, I'm glad to see that you two are getting acquainted.' Brant joined them and put an arm around each of them. He looked from one to the other and if he noticed the over-bright glitter of his wife's eyes he made no mention of it.

'Yes, and it's no thanks to you,' his mother returned crisply, but there was a glint of humour in her tone. 'You didn't even introduce us properly.'

'Didn't I?' Brant grinned. 'Well, Mrs Harcourt, I would like you very much to meet Mrs Harcourt.'

Helen rolled her eyes. 'I hope you know what you are

letting yourself in for, Kelsey, because my son is quite impossible.'

'Yes, I know,' Kelsey agreed quietly. She met Brant's dark sardonic gaze steadily. 'But I think I know how to handle him.'

Daniel came over to join them at that moment. He looked extremely stylish in a three-piece suit, a pink carnation in his lapel. He held out his hand to Brant. 'Congratulations, Brant.'

'Thanks.' Kelsey wondered if it was her imagination, or was Brant's tone a little dry?

'Do you mind if I kiss your bride?'

There was just a moment's hesitation. 'As long as you don't want to make a habit of it.' It was said in a joking manner, yet Kelsey sensed a slight edge to the reply. Before she had time to think about it, Daniel had moved towards her.

'You look gorgeous, Kel,' he murmured huskily. 'I'm as jealous as can be.' Then he bent his head and kissed her on the lips.

The kiss took her by surprise; she had expected him to kiss her cheek. Her skin flushed a little with embarrassment, and she was relieved to find when she looked up that some other people had come over to claim Brant's and Helen's attention.

'I hope you will be very happy, Kelsey.'

'Thank you.' Kelsey smiled up at her old friend. 'Maybe you'll take the matrimonial plunge next?'

'No chance.' He shook his head and there was a gleam of amusement in his eyes as he murmured dramatically, 'Not now that I've lost my one true love.'

Kelsey laughed. 'But you've kept your sense of humour, Daniel, that's the important thing.'

'Got to laugh or you'd cry,' Daniel said with a shake of his head. 'Talking of crying, I bet your friend over there did a lot of that last night.'

'Who?' Kelsey frowned, completely lost by this.

Daniel leaned closer and put an arm around her waist

as he whispered close to her ear. 'The beautiful Miss
Winters. If looks could kill you would have keeled over
at the wedding ceremony.'

'Oh. . .' Kelsey's eyes moved out across the room.
Susanna was standing with a group of men who worked
at the office. She was the centre of attention; they were
hanging on her every word. It was little wonder, because
she did look fabulous. Her dress was white with silver-
blue sequins, and it was the perfect foil for her lovely
figure and the silver blonde of her hair.

For a moment Kelsey was reminded of that picture of
Francesca in the magazine. There was a certain similarity
between the two women, she realised suddenly. Both had
a fashionably thin figure and a look of total sophistication.

'I probably shouldn't have mentioned her,' Daniel was
saying now. 'But I think you should watch your back,
Kelsey, you've made an enemy there.'

She returned her attention to him. 'Oh, I doubt it.
She has a whole host of admirers around her at the
moment. She's probably forgotten all about Brant and
me by now.' She forced a note of confidence into her
voice and gave him a bright smile. 'Thanks for worrying
about me, though.'

He grinned. 'You'd better just think of me as your big
brother from now on. That reminds me, did you get my
little gift?'

She frowned. 'What gift?'

Brant turned and interrupted them at that moment.
'Kelsey, it's nearly time we were leaving. Do you want
to go up to the room and change?'

A flurry of nerves and excitement shot through her as
she nodded, and her conversation with Daniel was
forgotten. Brant handed her the room key. 'I'll be up in
a moment,' he told her, before returning to his
discussion.

'I'll be back down soon.' Kelsey smiled up at her
friend before turning to leave the room.

The hotel bedroom was superbly luxurious. Kelsey

felt a momentary pang of regret that they were not going to stay here rather than jet off to some unknown destination.

She changed quickly, aware that Brant might walk in at any time and she didn't want him to find her undressed.

'You are ridiculous,' she told her reflection in the bathroom mirror. In a few hours' time Brant would see every inch of her and here she was worrying that he might catch a glimpse of her in silk underwear.

A delicious shiver raced through her as she remembered the way he had kissed her this afternoon, the way he had looked at her as she had stepped from the car, the red rose that he had sent. To Kelsey they were all symbols of Brant's deepening feeling for her. He might even be a little in love with her without realising it. She smiled, liking that idea.

She buttoned up her suit of midnight blue silk, put on the matching blue court shoes, and studied her reflection in the mirror. Her eyes sparkled and danced, her skin was flushed and radiant. She put up a hand to brush away some confetti that had insisted on staying in her hair, and a gleam of gold hit the light—her wedding-ring. She was married, she was Mrs Brant Harcourt. She said the name softly to herself and her heart lifted and sang with happiness.

She packed away her wedding dress in the case that was to go back to Brant's house. His mother had offered to take it back as she was staying at the house for a while before returning to England.

Everything done, Kelsey glanced at her watch. What on earth was taking Brant so long? Maybe he was being tactful by giving her plenty of time; he probably knew that she would be feeling a little shy of him. She was going to sit down and wait for him, then she changed her mind and decided to go and find him.

She heard his voice before she saw him. He was

coming out of the lifts at the far end of the corridor, and he wasn't alone.

'I know you don't love her. I could tell that you regretted the marriage as soon as the ceremony was over.' It was Susanna's voice and Kelsey felt herself grow cold as she came to a sudden and abrupt halt. She wanted to turn away, she didn't want to hear what they were saying, but for some reason she couldn't move; a grim kind of curiosity made her stand and listen.

'Kelsey is my wife, Susanna, and I——'

'Oh, I know that you're now going to be terribly noble about her. You're that type of guy,' Susanna cut across him anxiously. 'You'll try to do the right thing by her now, no matter how miserable it makes you.'

'Look, Susanna, my relationship with Kelsey is none of your damn business, so just butt out of it!' Brant sounded coldly angry. When he used that tone of voice it usually made people back down very quickly.

'Don't be cross with me, Brant, I can't bear it.' Susanna's mood turned tearful. 'I just wanted to talk to you about last night. I felt so upset after I left you, so confused. You were so——'

'I told you this morning to forget about last night.' Brant's voice was impatient. 'I don't want it to happen again; I think I've made myself clear on that score.'

'Yes.' Susanna's voice held a slight tremor.

Kelsey could tell that Brant was starting to walk away from her. If she didn't move now he would walk around this corner and straight into her.

'You know where I am when you need me,' Susanna called softly after him.

Kelsey had to go—she couldn't risk Brant seeing her—so she never got to hear what his reply had been. She ran quickly back towards their room. She could hardly fit the key in the lock because her hands were trembling so much. When she got inside she raced towards the bathroom and bolted the door behind her.

Then she leaned her head down into her hands and fought back the tears.

Snatches of Susanna's words rang in her ears. 'You don't love her. . .you regretted the marriage as soon as it was over. . . You were so. . .' So what? Passionate? Loving? Brant had spent the eve of his wedding in that woman's arms. Kelsey felt suddenly sick and light-headed, almost faint. She moved to the wash-basin and turned on the tap to splash her face with cold water.

There was a knock on the bathroom door. 'Kelsey, honey, what's taking you so long? We should be leaving now.' Brant's voice was gentle.

Kelsey had to take a couple of deep breaths before she could answer him. 'I'll be out in a moment.'

She rubbed her face with a soft towel and stared at her reflection. The eyes that stared back at her were lifeless, her skin distressingly pale. At least she hadn't cried; that would have been the final humiliation. Brant must not know that she had heard that conversation. It would serve no purpose to confront him with it. He would just tell her that it was none of her business what he did before he married her, and he would be justified in saying that. After all, he had made her no false promises of love; she knew why he had married her and she had accepted it. Anyway, it didn't sound as if Brant was going to continue the affair and he had told her that day in his office that he had no intention of having affairs once he was married, so there was no point in her making a fuss about something that was past.

'You'll try to do the right thing by her now, no matter how miserable it makes you.' Susanna's words felt as if they were branded on her heart. She didn't want Brant to be miserable—she wanted so much to make him happy.

'Kelsey, are you taking a bath?' Brant's voice sounded vaguely mystified now.

'No. I'm coming.' She turned away from her reflection and, taking a steadying breath, opened the door.

He was standing with his back to her, looking out of the window. He had changed, she noticed absently; his suit was a charcoal-grey and made from the finest quality slub silk. He turned and the dark eyes moved slowly over her, assessing every little detail of her appearance. 'Daniel was right when he said I was a lucky man. You look beautiful, Kelsey.' The velvet deep voice had a husky edge to it.

Kelsey suddenly wanted to cry; tears welled up inside her and burned in a raw aching way at the back of her eyes. Brant was saying what he knew she would want to hear. Susanna was right when she had said Brant would 'do the right thing'—he was that type of a man. He would look on it as his duty towards her to be kind, to pay her compliments when necessary. Even though he was not in love with her he would always take care of her.

'Is something wrong?' He took a step closer to her, a frown on his face.

'No. . .no, of course not.' She was trying so hard to put a brave face on things, for his sake as well as her own. 'Shouldn't we be going? We don't want to miss that plane.'

He nodded and took a few steps nearer. 'But first I would like to kiss my bride.'

Her heart hammered with a force that was painful as he reached for her. His kiss was slow and tender. It tugged at her heart-strings, it made her want to melt in against him. It made her want so much. . .

He lifted his head. 'I'm very tempted just to forget about that plane,' he murmured huskily. His gaze moved contemplatively towards the large double bed beside them. 'We could catch another one out tomorrow.' His eyes moved back towards her. 'What do you think?'

Kelsey wasn't really capable of rational thought at that moment. She wanted him to make love to her, but fear and apprehension were also racing wildly inside her. She didn't really know what she was frightened of. Was it

the fact that she was a virgin? Was it because Brant
didn't love her? Or maybe she was frightened that he
would compare her to the other women he had had in
his life and find her inadequate? It was a combination of
all these things, she realised suddenly, taking a hasty
step away from him.

'I think we should go, Brant. We have to go back
downstairs anyway, everyone will be waiting to say
goodbye to us.' She couldn't meet his eyes as she spoke.

'We don't have to do anything, Kelsey,' he told her
quietly. 'I'm sure all those people downstairs will understand perfectly if we don't go back down.'

'Yes, they probably will,' she conceded, but reluctance
ran heavily through the words.

There was an awkward silence. Kelsey didn't know
what he was thinking; she didn't dare to look at him.

He moved away from her and picked up the phone on
the bedside table. His back was towards Kelsey now and
she stared at the broad-shouldered frame, her heart
thudding anxiously.

'This is room 206. Could you send a porter up for our
luggage, please?' His tone was clipped and decisive.

Kelsey closed her eyes, relief tinged with regret somewhere deep inside her.

'Happy?'

Her eyes flew open as she realised he had addressed
this abruptly towards her. At this precise moment she
didn't think that she would ever feel happy again, but
she merely nodded. 'Thank you.'

He moved impatiently towards the door. 'Well, let's
get this show on the road, then.'

And that was exactly what it was, Kelsey thought a
little while later as everyone filed out of the hotel to wave
them off. And Brant played his part so well, the solicit-
ous, tender husband with his arm firmly around her
waist. It was little wonder that his mother had been
completely fooled into thinking her son was deeply in
love—the deception was brilliantly acted.

As the chauffeur-driven car pulled away from the crowds, Kelsey glanced back to wave. She could see Susanna standing slightly apart from everyone else. She was the only one who wasn't smiling and waving, she was the only one who guessed the truth. Their eyes met briefly and there was an expression on the coolly beautiful face that made Kelsey's blood run like ice through her veins. That look was filled with such unerring confidence that it said very clearly, 'Brant will come back to me, it's just a matter of time.'

The car rounded a corner and everyone was lost from sight.

They spoke very little on the way to the airport. Like her, Brant seemed lost in his own thoughts. She wondered what they were. Was he thinking about Susanna, or was he thinking about Francesca and how different things had been with her? She stole a few glances at him, but the hard rugged features were inscrutable.

They stood in the concourse at Lester B. Pearson airport, looking up at the flight-boards. London, Paris, New York. Kelsey's eyes moved over the different destinations and a glimmer of excitement stirred inside. 'Where are we going, Brant?'

He turned and smiled. 'Where would you like to go?'

She gave it some thought for a moment. 'Somewhere warm would be nice, where we could lie on a beach and just relax.'

He grinned. 'I was hoping you would say that. How do you feel about Florida?'

'Florida?' Her eyes lit up. 'Is that where we are going?'

'If it meets with your approval.' He reached out and took her hand. 'If you would prefer to go somewhere else it can be arranged.'

She shook her head and swallowed hard. She would have liked to have told him that anywhere with him would be wonderful. She would have liked to have fallen into his arms; she wanted so much to tell him how she felt, how much she loved him, how she only wanted to make him happy. But the words wouldn't come. Pride and the fear of rejection kept them locked deep inside. They stood slightly apart, silence between them, while all around the crowds swirled noisily.

He was the one who broke the strange kind of spell that held them. He squeezed her hand gently. 'Come on, let's go and chase after some sunshine.'

It was very late when they arrived at their destination, but Kelsey did not feel tired. They had flown directly to Miami and from there they had taken a light aircraft to Sarasota, where Brant had a car waiting for him. It had been a long journey, but, when Brant brought the car to a halt outside a large flood-lit house, Kelsey had never felt so alert. Butterflies had been dancing in her stomach since take-off in Toronto, and now that they had arrived they seemed to have exploded inside her in a riot of nervous energy.

Brant got out of the car and came around to open her door, but she had beaten him to it and was standing waiting for him at the boot of the car.

The night air was warm and fragrant with the scent of flowers. There was silence except for the gentle pounding of waves on the shore. She looked up at the house, illuminated against the velvet black of the sky. It was a Spanish colonial-style house with white arches leading out to a large patio. The patio and the steps leading up to the house were well lit, the lush gardens melted into dark shadow.

'I asked my cleaning lady to switch all the lights on as she was leaving,' Brant explained as he opened the boot of the car and took out Kelsey's suitcase.

'Is this your house?' She frowned. 'I thought we would be staying at a hotel.'

'No. This is my house.' He moved towards the steps and, as she didn't immediately follow him, turned to look at her. 'Is something wrong?'

'No.' She quickly moved to join him. Nothing was

wrong, unless you counted the fact that her heart was pounding so heavily against her chest that it was an actual physical pain. For some reason staying alone with him in a house seemed so much more intimate than the hotel suite that she had visualised. But then, no matter where they stayed things would inevitably be intimate.

Brant opened the door into a long entrance hall. Chandeliers blazed down on white walls and deep rose-coloured carpets. A door to one side led through to an enormous lounge. The furnishings were in keeping with the style of the house. Dark Spanish wood looked spectacular against plain white walls and copper-gold carpets.

Brant headed straight past the room and directly up the staircase. Kelsey followed at a slower pace.

The room that he showed her into was dominated by a huge four-poster bed. The water-silk covers echoed the turquoise carpets. A door to one side led through to an en suite bathroom.

Brant placed her suitcase down on the cushioned ottoman at the end of the bed, and then turned towards her. His eyes moved gently over the delicately pale face. 'Are you hungry, Kelsey?' he asked. 'You didn't eat very much on the plane.'

She shook her head and then promptly wished that she had lied. At least eating would delay things. 'I wouldn't mind a drink.' Her voice sounded slightly hoarse.

'Tea, coffee, or something stronger?'

'Something stronger.' Drinking in the early hours of the morning seemed decadent but right at this moment she was clutching at straws, hoping to gain some Dutch courage.

He smiled. 'All right. I asked Maria to put some champagne on ice. I'll bring it up.' He moved towards the door and then glanced back at her. She was standing just as he had left her, as if not quite sure what to do with herself. 'Make yourself at home, Kelsey. Have a bath or a shower if you want.'

'Thank you.' Her voice was stiff and formal as if she were speaking to a stranger. In a way that was what he was, she thought with rising panic, a stranger who was going to share her bed.

She moved towards her suitcase and opened it to rummage through it with shaking fingers. She found a long white silk nightdress and matching dressing-gown and took them into the bathroom, bolting the door behind her.

A hot bath did little to relax her. She took her time over it, drying her body slowly with the warm soft towels, rubbing lightly fragrant cream into her skin before reaching for the silk nightdress. It was a wrap-around style and she made sure the ties were very secure at the side of her slender figure before putting on her robe. She released her hair from the grips that had held it up and it tumbled in long shining curls around her shoulders.

She glanced briefly at her appearance in the mirror. Her skin was fresh and clear without its make-up. She looked younger than her twenty-eight years, and somehow vulnerable. She bit down on the softness of her lip. At this moment she wished fervently that she had not rejected the advances of her previous boyfriends, that she was more schooled in the art of making love. Brant would expect her to know how to please him; she would disappoint him.

She turned towards the bathroom door and her heart fluttered nervously.

As she had expected, Brant was sitting on the side of the bed. He was still fully dressed and looked totally relaxed, his dark head leaning back against the oyster-coloured satin headboard. His eyes moved over her slim figure in the flimsy silk nightwear, but he made no comment; neither did he comment on the length of time she had spent in the bathroom. He turned and lifted the champagne bottle from the silver ice-bucket, and deftly uncorked it to pour two sparkling glassfuls into long-stemmed crystal glass.

'Come here, Kelsey,' he directed gently as she continued to linger in the doorway.

She moved self-consciously towards him and sat a little distance away from him on the side of the bed. He handed her glass to her and she took it, careful not to let her hand touch his.

He raised his glass towards hers. 'To our life together.'

Was there an edge of mockery in that deep tone? She meant to just sip the champagne but instead she finished it with unladylike speed, hardly tasting its bouquet. She hesitated for a moment and then held out the glass for him to refill.

He took it but he didn't refill it; instead he put both glasses down.

'I would like another drink.' Her voice sounded vaguely imperious.

He smiled slightly. 'I know you would but I don't want you to have one. I want that lovely body of yours to be perfectly sober when I take possession.'

She flinched at that and her eyes darkened with pain. She stood up and moved away from him towards some sliding glass doors at the bottom of the room. They opened out on to a large balcony with steps leading down towards the beach. She slid the doors back to feel the fresh air against her over-heated skin. 'Do you have to say it like that?' she murmured softly. 'Couldn't you call it making love?'

'Taking possession, making love; it's the same thing.' There was a hint of impatience in his tone now.

'No, it's not, Brant.' She turned to look at him and her eyes glittered with an over-bright light, suggesting that tears were not far away. 'It's not the same thing at all.'

'Kelsey, I don't want an in-depth conversation. I want you,' he told her abruptly. 'Now, come to bed.' He got up and started to loosen his tie with impatient fingers as he walked towards her.

The purposeful light in his eyes made something inside her snap. Rational thought was gone and the fears that had been building up inside her came rushing to the surface. 'No!' Her voice trembled slightly but it was very forceful.

'Kelsey.' He reached out a hand towards her and she flinched away from him.

'Don't touch me, Brant.' Fear was clearly visible in her wide green eyes as she stepped back towards the open doors. 'I don't want you to. I don't want——'

'It's all right, Kelsey,' he interrupted her, but his voice was gentle now. 'Calm down. You are behaving irrationally. I'm not going to hurt you and I'm certainly not going to force myself on you.' He held out a hand towards her. 'Come away from those doors, you look as if you are about to flee into the night.' There was a note of wry humour in his voice, but it did little to lighten the tension inside her.

She knew that she was behaving foolishly, but she couldn't seem to help herself and the fear just wouldn't go away.

'Come on, Kelsey,' he said softly. He made no attempt to move towards her. 'You are just over-tired. You'll feel better after a good night's sleep.'

She did feel tired suddenly. She was emotionally drained. The last few weeks had taken their toll on her, plus the fact that she hadn't slept at all last night. The wedding today had used up every last ounce of courage and energy so that now all she was left with was her fears, her insecurity. Right now all she wanted was to go to bed and pull the covers over her head.

'I am tired,' she murmured. Her eyes moved towards the bed and then back to Brant apprehensively. 'You won't——' Her voice trailed off nervously.

'No, I won't,' he assured her drily, correctly interpreting her question.

Since she continued to hesitate, he moved away from her to turn back the covers of the bed. 'Get some rest, Kelsey. I can assure you that you are perfectly safe. I'm not about to pounce on you.' He turned away from her and took his jacket off to sling it across the nearest chair.

'Where are you going to sleep?' She swallowed to relieve the raw dryness in her throat as she stared at his broad shoulders in the white silk shirt.

He turned and one dark eyebrow rose sardonically. 'Right next to you in our marital bed, sweetheart. That is something that you will have to get used to. I thought I made myself clear abut that.'

'Yes. . .but I. . .' She broke off and just stared at him with wide, unconsciously pleading eyes.

He turned away and started to head for the bathroom. 'Get into bed, Kelsey. I've told you I won't touch you. What are you waiting for, an affidavit?'

'No, I——' The bathroom door closed on him, cutting her off in mid-speech. She stood there staring at it and had to swallow down the tears. She felt so foolish, so inadequate. She had made a real mess of things and she had wanted so desperately for things to be right. She heard the heavy jet of the shower as Brant turned it on and then moved to get into bed.

The silk sheets felt lovely next to her skin. She buried her head into the softness of her pillow and pulled them over her. Then she tried to think rationally about the day's events, about her behaviour.

She remembered the red rose that Brant had sent her and her lips curved into a smile. Then she remembered Susanna's words, 'I could tell that you regretted the marriage as soon as it was over.' She recalled that look in Brant's eyes just before he'd kissed her in front of all the watching crowds. There had been a glimmer of regret in those dark eyes. Scenes from the day flashed into her mind like pictures in a book. Suddenly she found herself remembering something that Daniel had said about a gift. She frowned—she couldn't call to mind any gift that she had received from him. It was only then that the truth dawned on her. That rose hadn't been sent from Brant, it had come from Daniel.

The shower switched off in the next room and she could hear Brant moving about. Then the bathroom door opened and he was back in the bedroom. Kelsey lay perfectly still; she was as far over her side of the bed as was possible and the covers were still wrapped protectively over her. She heard the light switching off. Then the mattress gave slightly as Brant got into bed. Kelsey squeezed her eyes tightly closed; she hardly dared to breathe, she felt so tense.

'For heaven's sake get some sleep,' Brant muttered. He adjusted his pillows and turned, then there was silence.

At some point Kelsey must have drifted off into an uneasy sleep. She dreamt about her wedding, but instead of the crowds watching her with approval they were all laughing at her, they all knew that Brant did not love her. Susanna stepped forward. 'You'll never keep a man like Brant satisfied,' she sneered. Then she could hear Brant's voice. 'I'm sorry, Kelsey, but I'm going to leave you.'

Her breath seemed to freeze in her throat and her eyes flew open. Her head was lying just beneath Brant's on the same pillow, and his hand was resting on the curve of her waist. It was a shock to find him so close. At some time during the night she must have moved, for she was now well and truly over on his side of the bed.

She tipped her head back to look up at him and then relaxed as she found that he was still asleep. Early morning light softened the strong features. It was strange but in sleep those features were not nearly so tough or intimidating; in fact there was something that was almost vulnerable about that handsome face now. A curious kind of ache seemed to be building up inside her. She swallowed hard and cautiously moved his hand so that she could slide back over to her own side of the bed.

She glanced over at him to see if her movement had disturbed him. He was still asleep. The turquoise silk sheets had slipped down nearly to his waist, revealing a torso that was bronzed and powerful. Her eyes moved over the dark whirls of hair on the broad chest, the strong arms, the narrow waist. The early morning light seemed to highlight the compelling, forceful power of his body. Kelsey found it hard to drag her eyes away from him and her breathing felt strangely constricted. She moved restlessly. She had read somewhere that men were more. . .amorous first thing in the morning. She darted another nervous glance at his sleeping profile and carefully slid out of the bed.

She picked up her white silk wrap from the chair beside her and crept cautiously towards the sliding glass doors.

It was a beautiful morning. The sun had risen, lighting the sky and the sea with fiery gold fingers. Kelsey walked to the edge of the balcony and looked down along the deserted beach. Palm trees fringed the white sand; they stirred and waved in the warm early morning breeze. She sighed deeply; this place was a tropical paradise, the ideal location for a romantic honeymoon. She bit down on the trembling softness of her lower lip.

She had behaved like a child last night, a scared, vulnerable child. If Brant had regretted having to marry her yesterday, then last night he must have deplored the move. Tears stung her eyes. She had wanted so much for things to be right that she had brainwashed herself into thinking that she would make Brant fall in love with her. The only thing that she had succeeded in doing was alienating him even further.

'What are you doing out here, Kelsey?'

Brant's voice startled her and she spun around to find him standing in the open doorway. He was only wearing the bottom half of black silk pyjamas. She averted her eyes from the powerfully attractive body and shrugged. 'Just admiring the view, I guess.' Did that remark sound as stupid as it felt? She stared out at the ocean, searching frantically through her mind for something to say to him. She had never felt so inadequate, so foolish, in all her life.

He moved and stood next to her, leaning his hands on the edge of the balcony as he looked out at the brilliant play of colours over the water. 'Beautiful, isn't it?' The deep voice sounded lost in thought. 'When you look out at a scene like that it makes you realise how small and inconsequential you are in the large scheme of things. Kind of puts any problems you might have into perspective, don't you think?'

She turned startled eyes on him. She couldn't believe that the tough, powerful Brant Harcourt ever felt inconsequential, let alone small!

He turned and caught the expression on her face and his lips curved in a wry smile. 'Even successful lawyers have moments of uncertainty, Kelsey.'

He was trying to make her feel better, she realised suddenly. She swallowed hard on a lump in her throat. She didn't want him to be understanding and gentle—somehow that made her feel worse about it all.

He turned his attention back to the ocean. 'I bought this place some time after Francesca's death. It helped me come to terms with a lot of things.'

And now he was coming to terms with a wife he didn't really want. Kelsey squeezed her eyes tightly closed. Brant had been through such a lot, he deserved to be happy now. He deserved better than this.

She took a deep breath. 'I'm sorry about last night, Brant. You've been very. . .good about it. A lot of men would have. . .would have. . .' She trailed off awkwardly, feeling embarrassed now and wishing she hadn't brought up the subject of last night.

'Would have taken what they wanted regardless of your objections.' He finished her sentence in a grim tone. 'Is that the kind of man that you think I am?'

'I don't know what kind of man you are,' she answered

truthfully. 'Sometimes I think that I do, then you say something or do something that completely throws me and I don't know where I am with you.' She stared out to sea and her voice was a mere whisper now. 'All I know is that there is no love between us and we have made a terrible mistake. I don't think I have been thinking rationally these last few weeks.'

'On the contrary, my dear Kelsey, your thoughts have been very sharp. To quote, "I can see that marriage to you might be a good deal for me."' His voice was icy.

Kelsey flinched as she remembered that cold conversation. She turned towards him, eager to tell him that she hadn't meant a single word that she had uttered that day. Then she saw the cold look on his face and realised that there was absolutely no point in telling him that. To do so she would have to admit that her mind was filled with romantic dreams and he would despise her for that. 'It's not too late, Brant,' she said instead. 'We could still get ourselves out of this mess.'

'And how do you propose we do that?' There wasn't a flicker of emotion on the hard features.

She swallowed. 'We could get the marriage annulled. As it has not been consummated I'm sure——'

'You are not sure about anything at the moment, Kelsey,' he cut across her abruptly. 'But I am, and there is no way our marriage will be annulled. You made a promise to me yesterday; those kind of promises are not easily broken, not as far as I'm concerned. I'm not going to allow you to just change your mind. There is far too much at stake for that.'

'Like the McConell shares, I suppose,' she flung back bitterly. 'That's the bottom line, isn't it, Brant? You don't give a damn about anything except the fact that you now have control of that precious business.'

'You knew the terms of our marriage when you agreed to it,' he answered drily. 'In fact you dictated a few terms of your own.'

'I know I did,' she snapped, angry that he should keep

reminding her about that. 'But it's one thing negotiating to give your body in a business deal and quite another putting the deal into practice.'

'So what you are actually saying is that you've got cold feet.' His mouth twisted in a lop-sided smile. 'Where is the woman who was begging me to make love to her a few weeks ago?'

Colour suffused her face. How could he be so cold, so unfeeling as to fling that moment at her like that?

'Of course, I had just given you a diamond and emerald necklace,' he murmured contemplatively. 'Was that where I went wrong last night?'

Without her even stopping to think about it, her hand swung back and she caught him a stinging blow to the side of his face.

As soon as she had done it she was horrified. She had never in her life struck anyone like that, let alone someone as daunting as Brant. 'Oh, Brant, I'm sorry.' Her hand fell to her side. 'I didn't mean to do that, it's just that you went too far.'

'On the contrary, I don't think I've gone far enough, that's the whole problem.' His voice was perfectly calm, but there was a look in his eyes that made panic rise very quickly inside Kelsey.

She made to step back from him but one strong hand effectively stopped her from moving. 'What are you going to do?' Her voice was a mere whisper.

'What I should have done last night.' He picked her up as if she were a flimsy rag doll and carried her back into the bedroom.

'This is crazy, Brant. Put me down at once.' Her voice wasn't at all steady. She could feel his hands on her skin through the soft silk of her gown and it was doing strange things to her body temperature.

He did put her down, but not until he had reached the four-poster bed, and then he flung her on to it, his manner none too gentle.

For a moment she just lay there staring up at him, her

eyes wide and frightened, her hair spread out on the turquoise covers like golden silk. Then, as he moved down towards her, she made a wild and frantic scramble to get off the bed. He caught her easily, pulling her back and then pinning her to the bed with the weight of his body.

'Stop it, Brant, stop it.' She pushed ineffectually against the broad shoulders. It was useless to struggle. As if she were a gazelle trying to fight off a lion, her movements were only a mild irritation to him. He caught both her hands in one of his and held them back above her head.

She moved her head to one side as his lips came down towards hers. 'If you do this, Brant, it will be rape.' Her voice shook. All she had left to fight him off were words.

He laced his free hand through her hair and pulled her face towards his. 'It won't be rape, Kelsey, I promise you.' Then his lips came down on hers, hard, hungry and very demanding.

It was humiliating how easily he could win her over. One kiss, that was all it took, then when he released her hands instead of fighting him off she was mindlessly reaching out for him, her hands loving the smooth satin feel of his skin, her lips responding wildly to his.

His lips moved down over the creamy length of her neck, then his hands were unfastening the ties of her nightwear. She made no attempt to stop him; she didn't want him to stop, she desperately wanted to feel her skin against his.

The silk slithered easily away from her body, leaving her totally naked. 'Brant.' She whispered his name huskily and her body moved gently, sensuously beneath his.

He moved back slightly from her and his eyes raked over her slowly, studying her every curve. Then his hands swept downwards, skimming the soft outline of her breasts. His eyes were dark with desire as they looked deep into hers. 'You're very beautiful, Kelsey

Harcourt.' His voice had a ragged unevenness that made her smile.

She held her arms up to him like a child waiting to be loved, and it was his turn to smile. 'What happened to my reluctant bride?' he asked teasingly.

CHAPTER SEVEN

THE sun beat down mercilessly on to Kelsey's fair skin. She knew that she should move out of it, but she didn't want to stir because she knew Brant was watching her and she knew that he was puzzled.

'Kelsey, did I hurt you this morning?' He was sitting on the lounger next to her and he stretched out one hand to gently smooth a strand of hair away from her face. The touch of his fingers against her skin sent a tremor of desire racing through her body. She lay very still and kept her eyes closed, hoping that he would think she was alseep; she didn't want to answer any of his questions.

'Kelsey, honey, don't fall asleep in this heat; you'll get badly burned.' He picked up a tube of her expensive sun-screening cream that sat next to them on the table and applied it liberally to the smooth bare skin of her back. The firm touch of his hand as he massaged it in sent pleasurable waves of delight racing over her skin. She murmured, torn between clinging to the pretence of sleep and the tantalising invitation of that touch.

She opened one eye and looked up at him. He had just come out of the shower; she could smell the clean scent of his soap and his hair was still wet. He wore a white towelling robe that emphasised the honey-burnished sheen of his skin. He looked so attractive that her insides seemed to tie themselves in knots. There should be a law against any man being so handsome, she thought idly.

'How do you feel?' He leaned forward and kissed her lips.

'Do you really want to know?' She opened both eyes and they sparkled mischievously as she leaned up to whisper in his ear.

'Good grief, woman.' He pretended to look shocked.

114

'At this rate I'm going to go back to work totally exhausted.'

She laughed and wound her arms up around his neck. For a while there was no further conversation as Brant took his time over a long and very thorough kiss. When he released her she lay back against the lounger feeling breathless, her heart beating out of all control.

He stared down at her for a moment, his dark eyes serious, unreadable. 'You didn't answer my question.' He returned to his original line of conversation, and she frowned.

It had been too much to hope that she had side-tracked him away from that subject. Brant's mind was far too keen, too alert to ever be distracted. 'What question was that?' she prevaricated, and lifted her hand as if to shield her eyes from the sun when in fact she was trying to hide them from him.

'Did I hurt you when I made love to you this morning?'

She smiled; at least he had called it making love and not taking possession. No word of love had been spoken, though, she recalled now; in fact they had hardly said more than two words to each other either during or after that passionate encounter.

'Only a little,' she answered truthfully, and then swung her legs over the side of the lounger to busy herself with rubbing cream into their long smooth length. She felt embarrassed by Brant's questions. She didn't want him to know that she had been a virgin and she didn't think she had done a bad job in trying to hide the fact. She had tried her best to please him and that skill had seemed to come naturally enough to her. She hadn't cried out when he had hurt her, and the pain had been lost quickly enough anyway because at that moment he had become very gentle, almost as if his body had recognised the fact that she was inexperienced.

'How long is it since you slept with someone, Kelsey?' he asked softly.

'Brant!' She turned large reproachful eyes up at him. 'What I did before we were married is none of your damn business. Besides, that is not the kind of question you should be asking a lady.'

Her voice sounded so prim and proper that he burst out laughing. 'Sorry, Kelsey, you're quite right, of course, it is none of my business. It's just that I know that you and Daniel were lovers and yet this morning I could have sworn that. . .' He caught the angry gleam in her eyes and grinned. 'OK, I'll shut up.'

'I should think so,' she muttered angrily, and rubbed the cream into her skin with a force that was painful. 'After all, I'm not questioning you about the last time you slept with somebody.' Probably because she already knew the answer to that question, she through grimly. Susanna Winters on the eve of their wedding.

'I hope you aren't planning to blame the bruises you are going to get on me,' Brant remarked drily as he watched her angry movements with the sun cream.

She stopped what she was doing and glanced down ruefully at the red marks on her skin.

'Are you hungry?' Thankfully Brant was the one who changed the subject.

She nodded. 'Ravenous.'

He smiled and hauled her unceremoniously to her feet. 'Then run along and slip into something. . .less comfortable.' He grinned as his eyes slid down her curvy figure in the brief bikini. 'Something less likely to give me high blood-pressure.' He turned her to face the sliding doors into the bedroom and lightly tapped her bottom. 'And I'll take you to a nice little restaurant that overlooks the sea.'

'Sounds wonderful.' She moved gracefully towards the doors and then turned. 'Brant?'

'Yes.' He had been about to pour himself a glass of iced water from the jug beside him, but he turned at her voice.

'I know we've agreed that what happened before we

married is not on the agenda for discussion.' She hesitated for a brief moment. 'But can I just ask you one question?'

'Ask away,' he replied lazily.

'Have you ever brought any of. . .your friends here?'

'I suppose by that you mean female friends?' She could hear the smile in his voice, but she didn't dare look at him. She knew she shouldn't be asking, it was really none of her business, but for some reason she just had to know.

'Yes,' she said quietly.

'No, I've always come here alone.' He crossed over towards her and tipped her head up with a gentle hand so that she was forced to look at him. 'Why do you ask?'

She shrugged self-consciously. 'Just curious.' She pulled away from him and he allowed her to turn and walk into the bedroom.

She opened the wardrobe and idly lifted out a couple of dresses that she had hung up earlier. Her mind wasn't on clothes, her heart was singing with happiness. She couldn't have explained to Brant her reasons for asking that question, but it had been very important to her. She wanted to think of this beautiful house as their special place. A place where there were no memories from Brant's past to intrude on them. No ghosts from the past, no worries about the future, just here and now. A tiny space of time where there was just her and Brant, an escape from reality.

As was always the way with life, you couldn't escape reality for long. It was waiting just around the corner, its long cruel fingers ready to snatch away the small piece of happiness that Kelsey had found. They were supposed to be away for two weeks, but in fact they only had nine days. Those days were the most wonderful in Kelsey's life. They lazed on the beach, swam in the warm clear waters, took a plane to the Everglades National Park and drifted through the mangrove swamps and watery

plains which teemed with tropical birds and alligators—
Kelsey even spotted a panther. It was when they arrived
home after that trip that the message was waiting for
Brant on his Telex machine.

Kelsey was in the kitchen plugging in the coffee
machine, and Brant had disappeared into his study. She
turned as he came in to join her.

'I really enjoyed today, Brant.' Her eyes sparkled and
she leaned back against the counter, looking totally
relaxed and very beautiful in the yellow sundress. It was
a shorter length than she normally wore and it showed a
lovely expanse of long shapely legs, now tanned to a
burnished gold colour. His dark eyes moved slowly over
her, the long legs, tiny waist, the soft swell of her
breasts. Her skin glowed with health; her long blonde
hair had lightened slightly in the sun and it gleamed with
silver lights.

Unaware that she was being studied so intently, Kelsey
turned to get some china cups from the cupboard behind
her. 'You do want coffee?' Her hair swung around as she
flung a questioning glance in his direction. 'Or would
you prefer something stronger?'

'I think I'd like a whiskey.'

'Oh.' She closed the overhead cupboard and bent in a
fluid supple movement to the drinks cabinet below. 'I
was thinking, I'd really like a trip to Disney World while
we're here. What do you think?' She poured him a
generous measure of whiskey and brought it over to him.

He didn't answer her immediately and she looked up
at him with a puzzled expression in her green eyes.
Usually when she suggested going somewhere he agreed
easily. 'If you don't want to go it's all right, it was just a
suggestion,' she told him quickly.

'It's not that I don't want to go, Kelsey, it's just that
we can't go.' He took his drink from her and put it down
on the table beside him. 'We have to go home tomorrow.
There was a message waiting for me on the Telex
machine. The date for the Sharman trial has been

brought forward. Susanna was assisting me with it but it's too major a case for her to deal with on her own. We'll have to fly back tomorrow.'

'I see.' Kelsey turned away from him, disappointment flowing through her. She busied herself pouring a cup of coffee. 'Well, it can't be helped, I suppose.' She tried to keep her voice light but it trembled alarmingly.

He moved to stand behind her and put his arms around her waist. 'We'll come back some time soon and I'll take you to Disney World.' He brushed back her hair and kissed the side of her neck. 'That's a promise.'

She squeezed her eyes tightly closed. She didn't care a damn about Disney World, she just didn't want their honeymoon to come to an end. She knew that once they got home she would be relegated to taking a back seat in Brant's life. Business was his priority, and then of course there was Susanna waiting in the wings. The very mention of that woman's name made her want to cry.

'Don't worry about it, Brant. I'm not really bothered; in fact it will be nice to get back to work.' She said the words she knew he would want to hear and was surprised to hear how convincing she made them sound.

He released her and moved over towards the kitchen phone. 'Such dedication,' he murmured, and there was an undertone to his words that Kelsey couldn't figure out.

'Who are you phoning?' she asked as he lifted the receiver.

'Thought I would give Susanna a buzz. Put her out of her misery and tell her I'm on my way to take over.'

'I'm sure that will be a big weight off her mind.' Kelsey's voice dripped with sarcasm. 'She's probably been worried sick about how she's going to cope all on her own.'

He slanted an amused look in her direction and she immediately felt very foolish. If she wasn't careful Brant would guess just how jealous she felt over Susanna Winters, and that would be very humiliating.

She glanced at her watch and tried to cover the awkwardness of the situation by changing the subject. 'Will there be anyone at the offices?' she asked, trying to work out the time difference.

'No, I'm ringing her at home.' Brant pushed the buttons without any hesitation and without having to look up the number. Obviously a number he was well used to ringing, Kelsey thought bitterly. She turned and poured her coffee down the sink, pouring herself a whiskey from the bottle she had left out.

'Hello, Susanna, Brant here.' His voice was warm and deep; somehow to Kelsey's ears it sounded far too intimate. He laughed at something she said. 'No, you did the right thing in contacting me. How long have you been trying to struggle with the case on your own?' One dark eyebrow rose in surprise. 'Really? You should have got in touch sooner.' He laughed again. 'No, we've been having a nice time here.'

Nice! Kelsey's brain seized the word angrily. She would have said they were having a wonderful, fabulous time; he just thought it was 'nice'. She swallowed the remainder of the whiskey in one gulp and poured herself another.

'Hold on a moment, Susanna.' Brant put his hand over the receiver. 'Be careful, Kelsey,' he cautioned in a low voice. 'That stuff can be lethal when you're not used to drinking it.'

She flung him a defiant look from ice-green eyes and took a long deep drink. She didn't even notice how it burned her throat as it went down. It was making her feel better—it dulled the storm of emotions that were churning around inside her.

'I haven't had a chance to study the material you've sent me yet. By the looks of things you're doing an excellent job.' Brant returned to his conversation. 'I'll look through it tonight and then we can go over it together when I return.'

Kelsey put her empty glass down and left the room.

She didn't want to listen to any more. On impulse she opened the sliding doors in the lounge and stepped out.

The night air was cool against her heated skin—it made her feel a little light-headed. She took a couple of deep breaths but that didn't seem to help. For a moment she stood, not quite certain what she should do, then she kicked off her shoes and walked down towards the beach.

There was something magical about walking along a beach at night. The only noise was the crash of the waves as they broke on the shore. A full moon sailed in and out between the clouds, plunging everything into deepest black and then into an unearthly silvery light.

Kelsey stared out to sea. She hated Susanna, but more than she hated that woman she hated herself. Jealousy was a detestable emotion. She loathed herself for allowing it to take over her whole body so easily. She tried to think sensible, logical thoughts. Of course they had to go home, the Sharman trial was very important. It was unfortunate that Susanna was the one who would be working on the case with Brant, but it wasn't the end of the world. Just because they would be working closely together it didn't mean. . . She didn't want to think what it might mean. Of course Brant knew her number, he had dated her a couple of times.

What would they be talking about now? She remembered the conversation that she had overheard on the day of her wedding and desperately she tried to push it out of her mind. Would Brant be telling her that he was bored, that he was glad of the excuse to go home? She could almost hear his voice saying those words. Yes, that was what he would be saying, she just knew it was. Jealousy surged through her like a red-hot tide. Moonlight blurred with the inky black of the sea as tears shimmered, ready to fall.

'Kelsey.' The deep timbre of Brant's voice startled her and she whirled around.

He was standing just a couple of feet behind her. He looked taller, somehow, in the shadowy light, his shoulders incredibly broad and strong. 'I'm sorry our time together here has to be cut short.'

To Kelsey's mind those words had a hollow ring. She shrugged. 'It's probably a good thing. I was beginning to get a little bored, anyway.' She was hurting and she wanted to hurt him.

'I didn't realise that I was boring you.' His voice had a harsh edge now and she knew that she had struck that dominant male pride of his.

'Well, it's not you exactly, it's just the situation. After a while it gets a bit monotonous when there's just two of you. It will be nice to get back to work and mix with other people again.' What are you saying, Kelsey? she screamed inwardly. She was making everything worse. But she couldn't seem to help herself.

'And is there any one person in particular that you are looking forward to seeing?' His voice was so cold that she felt herself shiver.

'No, not really.' She shrugged lightly. 'If you don't mind, Brant, I think I'll go in now. I'm feeling tired.'

She made to move past him but he caught her arm in a vice-like grip. 'But I do mind, Kelsey, I mind very much. I think you should stay out here and we can work on this bored feeling of yours. Try and spice things up a little for you.' He pulled her closer and with his free hand started to unbutton the top two fasteners of her dress.

'Brant, what on earth do you think you're doing?' She struggled violently to escape his hands, her voice trembling with anger.

'I would have thought that was pretty obvious, honey.' His voice was silky smooth and very calm as his hand lingered at the third button of her dress.

'But you can't.' Her voice was little more than a horrified whisper. 'Not here.'

'Why not?' A note of amusement crept into his voice now. 'It's my private beach—I can do what I want on it. There's no one around here for miles.'

'Now you're just being ridiculous.' She pushed at the broad chest in vain, then, as his hand continued to unfasten her buttons, she pulled away from him with all her strength.

Much to her surprise he relinquished his hold on her and she staggered backwards and over-balanced on to the soft white sand. For a moment she just lay there, stunned, her breath knocked from her body by the fall. Then, as he knelt down beside her, she struggled to sit up.

'That hurt!' She glared up at him with large reproach-ful eyes.

'Sorry.' The apology was made in a bland insincere voice, then the firm lips curved into a half-smile. 'If you tell me where it hurts I'll kiss it better.'

She opened her mouth to make some cutting reply, then caught the gleam of devilment in his eyes and leaned back in the sand. 'You are crazy, do you know that?' She tried to sound stern but laughter bubbled up inside her. How come he was able to make her cry, then laugh, with such insouciant ease? she wondered dream-ily. Then his lips came down, warm and gentle against the softness of hers.

She hardly noticed that his hands were unfastening the last of the buttons on her dress, not until it fell open and his hands ran down her neck then possessively cupped the naked curve of her breasts.

'You drive me crazy,' he growled in a low tone. 'Especially when you wear short dresses and very little underwear.' His lips moved downwards, following the same path as his hands. 'How's the boredom now, Mrs Harcourt?' he murmured huskily.

She didn't answer, she couldn't answer. Her brain had stopped functioning in any kind of a rational manner. There were no more words, only the fierce thunder of waves against the shore and the feel of Brant's skin against hers.

* * *

The only thing about living with your boss was that you couldn't easily skip a day at work. You couldn't ring up and make the usual kind of excuses over the phone, you had to look your boss in the eye as you made your little white lies. Kelsey wasn't the kind of girl who skipped work unless it was absolutely necessary and she was no good at telling lies.

She glanced nervously across the breakfast table at Brant. He was opening the morning mail. There was a stern look about him as he studied some legal-looking document that had been marked for his urgent attention. He looked unapproachable, distant, very much the successful lawyer, not the tender husband who held her in his arms at night. But then he hadn't held her very much lately. They had been home from their honeymoon for over a month now and during all that time Brant had seemed to treat her like some stranger who was lodging with him, not his wife.

Of course, he had been extremely busy since their return. The Sharman trial was proving to be very complex. He had managed to have the date for it put back again because of some new evidence that he had found, but he still found it necessary to sit up every night going over the details of the case well into the early hours. He looked tired, she noticed now, and there were lines of strain around his eyes.

'Brant.' She leaned across impulsively and touched the dark material of his jacket. 'Why don't we take some time off this weekend, go out somewhere?'

'Impossible.' He answered her without even glancing up from his letter.

Her lips tightened angrily and she withdrew her hand. He might at least have the decency to look at her when he spoke. 'You can't go on like this, Brant,' she continued, somehow managing to keep her voice calm and level. 'You're working far too hard. You know I could help you with some of that stuff you bring home if you——'

PLAYING BY THE RULES   125

'I've got all the help I need, Kelsey,' he cut across her drily, and then glanced over at her. 'Thanks anyway, it's good of you to offer,' he added, almost as an after-thought, as if suddenly realising how abrupt he had sounded.

'Don't mention it,' she murmured in a heavily sarcas-tic tone. 'Any time.' He wasn't listening to her; his attention was firmly back on his letter.

She glared at him. Of course he didn't need her assistance, not when he had Susanna Winters practically living in his office. Immediately that thought entered her head she firmly pushed it away. She wasn't going to dwell on that; it was probably what had been making her feel so ill these last few days.

That brought her back to her original train of thought. How was she going to get some time off work without having to tell Brant where she was going? For some reason she really didn't want him to know that she was going to see her doctor. He would probably think that she was a malingerer; after all, there wasn't much wrong with her. She was probably just a bit run down. Maybe she wouldn't bother going after all; a few extra vitamins might fix her up.

'Good morning.' Brant's mother came in to join them at the table, a bright smile on her attractive face.

'Morning, Helen.' Kelsey smiled warmly at the other woman and started to rise to her feet in order to get her mother-in-law some breakfast.

'Stay where you are, dear.' Helen placed a detaining hand on her shoulder. 'I keep telling you, I'm perfectly capable of seeing to myself. You mustn't run around after me.'

'But it's no trouble, honestly,' Kelsey protested.

'I know.' Helen patted her hand and smiled gratefully. 'But if you spoil me too much I'll never be able to settle back into my house in England.' She gave Kelsey a conspiratorial wink. 'You might never get rid of your interfering mother-in-law.'

'No one could ever describe you as interfering,' Kelsey answered firmly and sincerely. Helen had been a godsend over the last few weeks. She had kept Kelsey company on the long evenings when Brant was locked away in his study, and she had helped to ease the undercurrents of tension in the house. If she had noticed anything was wrong, and Kelsey was sure she had, she had made no direct references to it. 'I'm going to miss you when you go. I wish you would stay a while longer.'

'Why don't you, Mother?' Brant put away his post and joined the conversation. 'I hate to think of you in that big old house all alone.'

'It's ten years since your father died, Brant. I'm used to being on my own and I love being back in England near to my sister and friends.' She smiled at her son. 'But I always appreciate your asking me. Maybe when my grandchildren arrive I will feel differently.'

There was a brief look of displeasure on Brant's face. 'In that case you might be waiting a very long time,' he answered in a dry tone.

A shaft of pain hit Kelsey, more from the look on his face than from his words. She swallowed and looked away from him.

'Nonsense.' Helen reached cheerfully for the coffee-pot. 'Aren't you eating anything, Kelsey?' Her sharp eyes noticed the fact that her daughter-in-law had nothing in front of her except an empty cup and saucer. 'You should, you know; breakfast is a very important meal.'

'I'm not really hungry,' Kelsey answered truthfully. 'I never seem able to face breakfast.' Before she could stop her, Helen had leaned across and was filling her cup. The smell of freshly ground coffee rose to assail her. Nausea swept over her in awful waves and she pushed the cup away hurriedly, spilling some of its contents on to the snowy-white tablecloth.

'Are you all right, dear?' Helen's eyes noted the chalk-white pallor of Kelsey's skin with some concern.

'Yes, perfectly; I just seem to have gone off coffee recently.' She looked ruefully at the stain on the cloth. 'I'm sorry about the tablecloth.'

'Kelsey, darling, it's yours, why are you apologising?' Helen got up and came around to kiss the side of her cheek. 'Sometimes I think you forget that this is your home now,' she said in a gentle tone. 'Now, how about some freshly squeezed orange juice?'

'Thanks, Helen.' For once Kelsey sat and allowed the other woman to wait on her. She felt dreadfully tired, probably because she hadn't slept very well last night.

'I think you should take the day off work, Kelsey,' Brant said suddenly. His eyes raked over her in a way that made her feel very uncomfortable. 'You don't look very well.'

'Good idea.' Helen bustled back in and put the orange juice down in front of Kelsey. 'You have been looking very peaky these last few days—it will do you good to stay at home.'

'Right, well, seeing as that's settled I'll get off to work.' Brant started to get to his feet.

Kelsey frowned, she hated to feel as if she were being rail-roaded into something. 'On the contrary, nothing has been settled,' she told him stubbornly. 'I have far too much on at work to be able to take a day off.'

Brant glanced down at her, seemed about to argue the point, then just shrugged. 'As you wish.'

Later, as she sat at her desk, she wondered why she had said that. Why hadn't she just taken the day off? It would have been the perfect opportunity to escape off to the doctor without Brant knowing.

As the morning wore on she felt worse, not better. Her head ached, her throat felt dry; she was definitely coming down with some kind of bug. She thought of the fresh orange juice that Helen had made for her with longing, and pressed the intercom through to her secretary. 'Does the machine in the corridor do fresh orange juice, Maggie?'

'Afraid not, Kelsey. Would you like your mid-morning coffee now?'

Kelsey's stomach turned over at the very thought. 'No, thank you.' She hesitated for a moment, then asked, 'How many appointments have I got for this afternoon?'

'Five. Woods, Kemp——'

'It's all right, Maggie, you needn't go through them. Get me an outside line, will you?' Kelsey flicked through her diary to find her doctor's number. She would try and get a lunchtime appointment and if she was late back then it was just too bad.

Luckily the doctor was able to squeeze her in, though the receptionist warned her that he might keep her waiting; he had a busy schedule.

She had just put the phone down when Daniel came into the outer office. She smiled at him through the glass partition and motioned for him to come through.

'Have you got a few moments, Kelsey?' He popped his head around the door.

'Of course. Come in. I've always got time for you.'

'Now, I wish that were true.' He grinned at her and sat down in the chair opposite. As usual he was dressed stylishly: the dark grey suit was tailored perfectly to his broad shoulders, a designer's insignia printed boldly on his silk tie. He swept a hand through his hair but it didn't move an inch out of place. 'Just wondered if you had thought any more about the offer I made for your grandfather's house?' he asked casually.

She bit down on the softness of her lip. 'Daniel, I'm so sorry. I meant to discuss it with Brant and I completely forgot.'

'That's OK, I'm in no hurry,' he replied easily. 'But do you think I could take your keys again to go and have another look around?'

'Yes, of course.' She reached for her handbag. She still had the keys to her grandfather's house, plus the keys to her old flat, which she hadn't yet sold, on her ring. She selected the relevant one and handed it across. 'So you are serious about buying it?'

He nodded. 'I'm getting a little tired of the bachelor-pad.'

'Does that mean you are getting tired of the bachelor way of life?' She grinned.

He hesitated and she laughed. 'Silly question.' The light on her phone flashed and she picked it up, the laughter still in her voice as she said her name.

'You sound very cheerful.' It was her husband's dulcet tone. 'I was just wondering if you were free for lunch.'

She was so surprised by the invitation that she didn't answer immediately. Brant hadn't asked her out for lunch since before they were married. That he should choose today when she had made that damn doctor's appointment really upset her.

'Are you still there?' He sounded vaguely amused.

'Yes, I'm here.' Her mind whirled frantically, trying to come up with some excuse to give him. Her eyes lighted on Daniel. 'But I'm sorry, Brant, I've just told Daniel that I would have lunch with him. We have a few things to discuss——'

'All right, Kelsey, another time then,' he cut across her drily. 'Speak to you tonight.' Then the line went dead.

Kelsey replaced the receiver regretfully, her mind so preoccupied that she almost forgot about Daniel.

'So where are we going for lunch?' he asked with a grin.

She grimaced. 'Sorry about that, Daniel. It's just that I have an appointment this afternoon and I didn't particularly want to tell Brant about it.'

'Oh?' One dark eyebrow rose. 'That sounds interesting, do you want to tell me about it?'

She hesitated; if she told him she was going to her doctor he would probably put two and two together and come up with six. It would be all over the office that she was pregnant or something. If she didn't tell him anything he would assume that she was having an affair—she knew what lines Daniel's mind ran along. 'Well, actually I'm shopping for a surprise present. I didn't buy Brant a gift when we were married so I want to look for one this afternoon.'

'Oh.' He looked slightly disappointed. 'Well, don't worry, your secret's safe with me.'

'Thanks, Daniel.' She smiled at him gratefully.

'That's all right. I'll probably go out and look at Joe's house at lunchtime, so no one will be any the wiser.'

Kelsey didn't go back to work after she had seen her doctor. Instead she phoned Maggie, told her that she was unwell and was going straight home to bed. Then she did exactly that.

She was relieved to find that Helen was not home. She didn't walk to talk to anyone. She went straight up the stairs to her bedroom, stripped off her clothes and got into bed, pulling the silk sheets over her head. Then she allowed the tears to fall. She wept copiously, stifling her sobs into the cool softness of her pillow. She had never felt so frightened in all her life.

CHAPTER EIGHT

MUCH to Kelsey's surprise, she realised that she must have slept, for when she opened her eyes the light was fading in the room. She sat up, pushing her blonde hair back off her face. Immediately her thoughts returned to her time with Dr Michaels and panic returned in full force.

She leaned against the softly padded headboard and tried to think calmly. The doctor hadn't been sure about anything; they wouldn't know for certain until the results of her test came through. She could be worrying unnecessarily.

She got out of bed and put on her white kimono, then sat down at her dressing-table to study her reflection. She looked a lot better than she had done this morning, she noted with some satisfaction. Colour had returned to her cheeks, in fact her skin had a kind of luminiscent glow about it as if she had spent the afternoon walking in the fresh air, not tucked up in bed. That sleep had probably done her the world of good, she thought cheerfully. Maybe lack of sleep had been her problem and Dr Michaels had been way off course with his diagnosis. The awful thing was that as it was Friday she would have to wait until after the weekend before she would know for sure. She didn't think that she could bear the suspense. With a heavy sigh she got up to make the bed and then went for a shower.

She changed into a blue cashmere dress and glanced at her reflection in the full-length mirrors on the wardrobe. She looked slim and elegant, no sign of the turmoil that raged within, which was strange because she had this horrible feeling that Brant would take one glance at her and he would know. It was a ridiculous thought.

Brant was so preoccupied with work that he probably wouldn't notice even if it was stamped on her in three-inch-high scarlet letters.

The house was strangely silent and dark. Kelsey flicked on the lights as she went downstairs. Obviously Helen wasn't home yet. She hoped she wouldn't be long; at this moment she felt as if she really needed the company of the other woman. Not that she could confide in her; that wouldn't be fair to Brant.

She went into the lounge and stood by the windows, staring out into the gardens. The scene looked cold and bleak; winter had overtaken the autumn, and there were no leaves left on the trees. Long shadows from their gnarled and twisted branches stretched over the drive as darkness closed in.

Kelsey pulled the curtains and switched on the lamp beside her. Then she knelt to light the fire. The warm crackle of burning logs was the only sound in the room. Kelsey sat back in the settee and stared into the bright orange flames.

She found herself thinking about her own mother. She wished that she were here now. It was at times like this that a girl needed her mother. Her lips curved in a sad smile; she had made that very same wish on numerous occasions over the years. Why did she always yearn for the impossible? Like wishing that Brant would fall in love with her when he clearly never would.

She remembered that day when he had brought her home for dinner and they had both sat here by the fire. She had caught a glimpse of a warm, relaxed Brant that day and she had fallen even more hopelessly in love with him. That time seemed so long ago. A lot had happened since then. Her name had changed, her home had changed, even her status at work, as Brant had fulfilled his promise and made her a junior associate. One thing had remained the same; she was still hopelessly in love.

She curled her legs up on to the settee and bent her head into her hands as despair washed over her. She wanted so much for Brant to return her love, but each day that possibility seemed more and more remote. In fact, since they had returned from their honeymoon, Brant seemed to have been deliberately distancing himself from her. Even when they made love and were as close as two people could get there was no real closeness between them. Afterwards Brant would move away from her and she was always left with the feeling that, although she had satisfied him physically, she had failed to satisfy him in a deeper, more meaningful way. That knowledge made her feel awkward around him. She never knew what she should say, how she should act. There was such a thing as trying too hard to please someone and that was what she was doing. The result was that her manner towards him was as stiff, formal and polite as his was to her. They were like two strangers who shared the same bed.

The sound of a car engine roused her from the depths of depression. She glanced at her watch; it was five o'clock—too early for Brant. They never got home from the office until nearly seven. It would probably be Helen.

She heard the front door open and close and she called out cheerfully, 'I'm in the lounge, Helen.'

The door opened but it wasn't Helen who entered, it was Brant. 'You're home early!' She swung her legs down from the settee and slipped her shoes back on, feeling suddenly self-conscious.

He made no reply to that; instead he asked coolly, 'Where have you been all afternoon?' He crossed the room and stood with his back to the fire looking down at her. Although his voice was calm and level there was an edge to it that told her very clearly that he was displeased.

She wondered what he would say if she told him exactly where she had been and what had been said. A dull flush spread up into her cheeks at the very thought. 'I'm sorry about the appointments I missed, Brant.' Her voice had a slight huskiness. 'I really didn't feel very well this afternoon. I had to come home.'

The dark eyes noted her heightened colour, the bright glitter of her eyes. 'You're a very poor liar, Kelsey,' he remarked in a dry, almost detached kind of voice.

She swallowed hard. 'I'm not lying, Brant, and I don't know why you should think I am.' He couldn't know anything about her trip to the doctor, he just couldn't, she thought wildly.

'So. . .what exactly is the matter with you?' He drawled the question out in a way that sounded very laid-back, but Kelsey knew that he was perilously near to losing his temper. She had never experienced the full lash of Brant's temper—he was always perfectly in control. She remembered how she had longed once to stir him into anger, how she had thought it preferable to that cool, icy manner of his. That thought seemed ludicrous now. The full force of Brant's wrath was a terrifying prospect.

'I. . . I don't know. I think I've just picked up a bug or something.' She got to her feet. She didn't like having to look so far up at him; it was unnerving her.

'Really?' One dark eyebrow rose disdainfully. 'But it didn't stop you having lunch with Marsden?'

She was lost now, she just didn't know what to say. 'Well, yes, it did, actually,' she mumbled finally. 'I cancelled lunch with Daniel and came straight home.'

'Now, that's strange,' Brant murmured and his tone was icy now. 'When Marsden deigned to come back into the office at four o'clock he told me that he had had a most enjoyable lunch with you.'

All the colour drained away from Kelsey's face now. She could have tried to offer him some excuse but she knew that that would only make matters worse. As Brant had so rightly said, she was no good at lying. She had told him one tiny untruth and he had caught her out immediately; if she told another he would just tie her into knots. It had been crazy to lie to a man who was a master at cross-examination. 'OK, counsellor, so I've been caught out.' She desperately tried to lighten the atmosphere. 'What do you think I'll get, ten to twelve years? Or do you think I might be let off with a promise of good behaviour?'

He wasn't amused; the dark eyes were intense, almost brooding as they stared down at her. 'Don't be flippant, Kelsey, it doesn't suit you.'

'Well, I don't know what to say to you.' She raked an impatient hand through her hair. 'So I told a little white lie and took the afternoon off work; it's hardly a mortal sin.'

A brief look of utter contempt flickered over the hard features, but he said nothing for a few minutes. Instead he walked over towards the drinks cabinet and poured himself a large whiskey. 'So how long has it been going on?' he asked in a gravel-hard voice.

She frowned, genuinely perplexed. 'How long has what been going on?'

'For heaven's sake, Kelsey!' The glass thudded down on the polished surface of the cabinet with a force that by rights should have shattered the delicate crystal. 'Do I need to spell it out to you? I know about your affair with Daniel Marsden.'

'You know what?' Kelsey's mouth literally fell open. She was so stunned that for a moment she couldn't find her voice. 'Brant, I don't know where you got such a ludicrous idea! I'm not having——'

'There is no point in denying it, Kelsey,' he cut across her coldly. 'Because if you think I give a damn, then you're sadly mistaken. All I'm concerned about is that you be a little more discreet in future. I don't want to have to deal with that kind of gossip at the office.'

'I see.' Her voice was low and calm, but inside she felt as if she were being torn apart by a thousand razor-sharp knives. Brant really didn't care about her at all.

He tossed back the remainder of his whiskey and then headed for the door. 'I'm going upstairs to shower and change. I have a dinner appointment this evening.' His voice was matter-of-fact, as if the previous conversation had never taken place. The door closed quietly and firmly behind him.

Stinging tears of pain welled up inside her but she fought them down; she refused to cry. She sat back down on the settee and tried to think clearly, but all she could do was remember Brant's words. 'If you think I give a damn, then you're sadly mistaken.' They chased round and round her brain in tormenting circles.

'There you are, Kelsey.' She jumped at the sound of Helen's voice; she hadn't even heard her opening the door. 'You're home early, aren't you?'

Somehow Kelsey managed to turn and smile at her mother-in-law. 'Actually I've been home all afternoon. I haven't felt well all day.'

'Really?' Helen frowned with concern and came to sit in the chair opposite. 'You do look very pale, Kelsey. You shouldn't have gone into work at all today.'

'Ain't that the truth!' Kelsey murmured in a bitter tone. Then, catching the puzzled look on Helen's face, she quickly changed the subject. 'You've been shopping, I see.' She indicated the carrier bags that had been put down next to her chair.

'Yes, I've bought myself a lovely new outfit.' Helen grinned at her. 'And then I saw this exquisite dress and thought immediately of you.' She picked up one of the bags and handed it over to her.

'Helen, you shouldn't have!' Kelsey murmured, overcome by such kindness. She opened the gilt-edged box and took the dress out from the layers of tissue. The dress was the most beautiful creation that Kelsey had ever seen, blue-green silk inlaid with delicate bands of mother-of-pearl. It shimmered as it caught the light. 'It's fabulous,' Kelsey breathed in delight.

'I thought you would like it.'

'I love it.' Kelsey got up to kiss Helen's cheek, then

she held the dress up to her figure to study the effect in the large mirror at the end of the room.

At that moment Brant came into the room. His eyes moved coolly over the delicate beauty of the dress in a sweeping glance, but he made no comment. 'Thought I heard your voice, Mother.' His eyes moved towards Helen and Kelsey noticed how warm they were compared with the way he had looked at her. 'Have you had a nice day?'

'Yes, I have.' Helen smiled at her son. 'What do you think of Kelsey's dress?'

Dark eyes moved back towards her, but instead of moving down over the dress they lingered on the pallor of her skin.

'She will look beautiful in it, don't you think?' Helen prompted.

'Kelsey always looks beautiful.' He said the words that were expected of him and for some reason they lashed at Kelsey's heart. He looked devastatingly attractive in a dark evening suit. She wondered where he was going and, more importantly, whom he was going with.

'Do you think you will be late home?' she found herself asking suddenly.

'Probably. Don't wait up.' With a brief smile which encompassed them both, he left them.

Kelsey flinched as the door closed behind him. For one unbearable moment she was seized with a longing to run after him. She wanted to throw herself into his arms and beg him not to go. She turned and forced herself to smile at her mother-in-law, and it took every ounce of strength that she possessed to say calmly, 'Well, looks like there is just the two of us for dinner tonight.' She was unaware that her eyes were filled with an anguish that tore at Helen's heart.

Despite the fact that Helen was such wonderful company, the evening seemed to drag. Again and again she glanced at the time and wondered where Brant was. What he was doing? It was a relief at ten o'clock to make her excuses to Helen and escape to her bedroom. Then she lay in the darkness and tortured herself with images of Brant kissing Susanna. He was out with her, she just knew he was. He was probably quite happy to go on believing that she and Daniel were having an affair because it gave him an excuse to be with her.

At half-past eleven she heard Helen coming up to bed. Then the house was silent. Every minute seemed like an eternity. Then, at midnight, she heard the sound of his car. She lay and waited for him to come to her, but he never did. Finally, in the early hours of the morning, she fell into an uneasy sleep.

It was the sound of the bedroom door opening that woke her. 'Brant?' She struggled to sit up.

'I'm sorry, Kelsey, did I wake you?' It was Helen who came into the room. 'I only meant to peep round the door and see if you were all right.'

'I'm fine.' It wasn't strictly the truth. She felt unbearably tired still and her head ached. 'What time is it?'

'Nearly eleven.' Helen came and put a glass of orange juice on the bedside table, then she sat on the edge of the bed.

'Really?' Kelsey sat up. 'I never usually sleep so late.'

'You must have needed it,' Helen answered kindly. 'You look a little better than you did yesterday, but you're still very pale.'

'I probably just need some fresh air,' Kelsey said lightly.

'Maybe.' Helen's eyes moved to the other side of the bed and Kelsey knew that her sharp gaze had noticed that Brant had not slept there. 'I think that both you and Brant are working too hard. Brant was already in his study when I went downstairs at eight this morning.'

Kelsey swallowed hard. 'I think he spent most of the night in there, Helen. The Sharman trial comes to court next week so he's probably been going over the details of the case again.' Her voice sounded as flat as she felt.

She knew damn well that Brant hadn't come to bed last night because he hadn't wanted to sleep with her.

Helen patted her hand. 'When this case is over you should both take some time off. You know, Kelsey, despite what the romantics of this world say, the first year of marriage can be quite a tough period. It's not all hearts and flowers; it takes time to adjust to each other. After years of being single you have to learn how to share your life with someone else, and that isn't always easy.'

Kelsey took a deep breath. 'Is it very obvious that we are having problems?'

'Only to a blind man.' Helen smiled. 'Don't worry about it, Kelsey. You love each other and that is all that matters. You'll work it out.'

'You think so?' Kelsey sounded as dubious about that as she felt. That was just it; Brant didn't love her. Their marriage was a sham, it had hit one rough patch and already it was disintegrating around them.

'I know so,' Helen answered firmly. 'You just need time alone together. Which is one of the reasons I booked my flight home yesterday.'

'Oh, no, Helen!' Kelsey protested quickly. 'We love having you here——'

'I know you do, but I've encroached long enough on the newly-weds,' Helen cut across her and then smiled. 'Besides, winter is closing in here and at my age snow has ceased to hold any appeal.' With a conspiratorial wink at her daughter-in-law, she got up to leave the room.

'Helen.' Kelsey's voice halted her at the door. 'Thank you for everything. I'm really going to miss you.'

Helen left on Sunday. They both went to the airport to see her off and it was a sad occasion.

'I hate saying goodbye,' Kelsey murmured as they left the airport.

Brant flicked a glance down at her, but he said nothing. He probably felt worse than she did, Kelsey thought suddenly; after all it was his mother they had just said goodbye to. Impulsively she tucked her arm through his. 'Why don't we both go and have lunch out somewhere? Cheer ourselves up.'

'I have to go into the office.' His reply was blunt.

She dropped her arm from his self-consciously, feeling more than a little hurt by his coldness. 'Even the Prime Minister takes time to eat and sleep, Brant,' she murmured, and there was more than a little bitterness in her tone.

'You're not very quick on the uptake, are you, Kelsey?' he said in a hard voice. 'I don't want to have lunch with you.'

'I see.' Pain formed a hard, tight knot around her heart. They reached his car and he unlocked the central locking system so that they both got in at the same time. 'So where do we go from here?' Her voice was very unsteady.

'I thought I'd drop you back home and go on——'

'That's not what I meant, Brant, and you know it!' She rounded on him and her green eyes sparkled furiously in the pallor of her face. 'You don't want to spend any time with me. As you haven't come to our bed for the last couple of nights I can only presume that you no longer want to sleep with me. Is this something to do with my supposed affair with Daniel, or are you just plain tired of me?'

He turned to look at her and there was no glimmer of any emotion on the hard lean features. 'Bored is the word *you* like to use, if I remember correctly.'

She closed her eyes, her pain increasing to an almost intolerable level. She had her answer.

Brant started the car engine and they drove home in silence. It wasn't until they pulled up outside the house that Kelsey felt strong enough to speak to him without breaking down into tears. 'Just for the record, I am not having an affair with Daniel.' She spoke quietly.

The look he gave her was filled with disbelief.

'Why are you so keen to believe the worst of me, Brant?' Her voice held only a slight tremor to hint at the trauma inside. 'Is it because you think that if I'm not playing by the rules of our marriage then it's easier for you to break them? It's easier for you to do what you want, see who you want without feeling guilty?'

'I have no reason to feel guilty, Kelsey. As you so succinctly put it, you are the one who has broken the rules.' He glanced pointedly at his watch. 'I have an appointment, so if you wouldn't mind.' He stretched across her and opened the door.

'I do mind, Brant,' she said in a tightly controlled voice as she got out. 'I mind very much.'

The Rolls accelerated with a speed that was frightening, down the drive and out on to the road.

The first thing that Kelsey did when she arrived in her office on Monday morning was to phone her doctor.

'Ah, Kelsey!' Dr Michaels' tone was warm and friendly. 'Yes, I have the results of your test in front of me. I'm very pleased to tell you, my dear, that my diagnosis was correct, you are indeed pregnant.'

'I am?' The room seemed to whirl around her in an exciting jumble of colours.

'Yes, congratulations to you and your husband. I'll switch you through to my receptionist and perhaps you will book another appointment to come and see me?'

'Yes. . .yes, of course.' Kelsey went through the whole procedure in a kind of daze. Even when she put down the phone she sat staring into space. She could hardly believe it, she really was pregnant.

Last night when she was lying alone in her bed she had tried to think clearly about what she would do if her tests proved positive. She hadn't been able to make any kind of a decision. The only thing that she knew for certain was that Brant would not want their child. He had made that very clear before they had married.

She placed an instinctively protective hand down on

to the still flat planes of her stomach. She wanted this baby, she realised suddenly, she wanted it with a fierceness that startled her. The fear that had raged through her all weekend had quite suddenly abated. Brant's reaction to the news of her pregnancy was no longer her prime concern. Her baby came first now and she would have it with or without Brant's approval. Probably without, she realised dully.

She raked an agitated hand through long blonde hair. Now that her pregnancy was confirmed she would have to tell him. She balked at the very thought. She didn't feel strong enough to cope with Brant's reaction to the news. Maybe in a couple of weeks, after she had had time to think everything through.

'Kelsey, your first appointment has arrived. Mrs Woods; shall I sent her in?' Maggie's voice cut into her thoughts.

'Yes, please.' Taking a deep breath, Kelsey opened the files in front of her and tried very hard to push all her problems to the back of her mind.

CHAPTER NINE

'Is IT all right if I go now, Kelsey?' Maggie asked, popping her head around the office door.

Kelsey glanced at her watch, startled to find that it was nearly six-thirty. 'Yes, of course. I'm sorry, Maggie, I didn't realise it was so late.'

'That's OK,' her secretary answered brightly. 'It's just that I want to go home and start preparing for our big evening.'

Kelsey nodded, but she couldn't hide her obvious lack of enthusiasm; she was in no mood for a party.

'Well, I'll see you tonight, then.' Maggie hovered in the doorway, a look of puzzlement in her clear grey eyes.

'Yes, see you tonight.' Kelsey managed to inject a note of geniality into her voice and then gave a sigh of relief as her secretary turned to go. She left both of the office doors open as she left and the sound of music drifted from the waiting-room across the corridor.

Kelsey tried to ignore the cheerful strains of 'Jingle Bells' and 'Rudolf the Red-nosed Reindeer' as she turned her attention back to her work. It was ridiculous; Christmas seemed to get earlier every year. It was only the last week in November and already the preparations for the festive season had reached fever pitch. Having the firm's Christmas party tonight was also ludicrous, but then Brant had scheduled it early because he had to leave for Vancouver soon. She made a mistake in the report she was filling out and scored her pen heavily through it. Impatiently she opened the drawer beside her and pulled out a fresh sheet of paper to start again.

Today had been one of those days when nothing seemed to go right. It hadn't been helped by the fact that she had felt sick from the moment she had climbed out of bed this morning. But then, she should be used to that by now. In the last three weeks, since her pregnancy had been confirmed, she seemed to have spent most of her time feeling nauseous.

From the far end of the corridor Kelsey could hear a man's voice wishing someone goodnight. Very soon she would be the only one left in the building. Resolutely she started to write; the sooner she finished this, the sooner she could get home.

Home, the word echoed around her mind. Strangely enough Brant's house did feel like home to her now, even though her husband was more of a stranger to her than he had ever been. She hardly saw anything of him these days. He was heavily involved in the Sharman trial and that meant that he left the house before her every morning and at night he spent most of his time sequestered in his office. On the few occasions when he had come up to sleep next to her he had made no attempt to touch her. Those nights had been pure torture; she had lain awake aching to go into the warmth of his arms, yet she knew to do so would be to invite rejection.

She glared down at the paper in front of her. The situation had its compensations, she told herself grimly. If Brant had spent any more time around her he could not have failed to notice how sick she was every morning. Then it would only be a matter of time before he put two and two together. At least this way she could choose her own time to tell him.

The music from across the corridor stopped and the office was unnaturally silent. Kelsey read back over what she had written. Not surprisingly it was full of mistakes. 'Damn!' Her voice was unnaturally loud in the silence as she scrunched the paper into a tight ball and flung it at the waste-paper bin.

'Having problems?' Brant's deep voice coming from the doorway startled her.

Wide green eyes swung up towards him. 'You made

me jump.' Her voice was faintly accusing. 'I thought you
would have gone home ages ago.'

'Strange, I was about to say the same thing to you.'
He moved further into the room. 'Don't you think it's a
little impolite for a hostess to be late for her own party?'
he asked in a dry tone.

She glanced at her watch. It was seven o'clock; she
was cutting it very fine. People were due to arrive at
their house around eight. 'I won't be late,' she assured
him in a clipped decisive tone. 'Besides, as you put it so
succinctly last week, all I have to do is put on my dress
and play being your hostess for the evening—anyone
could do it.' A little of the bitterness that she had felt
when he had said those words spilled out into her voice.
That statement had hurt her a great deal. She didn't
think she was playing at being his hostess, she *was* his
hostess, his wife, whether he wanted her or not.

He frowned. 'I said those words to reassure you that
you wouldn't have any extra work put on you, not to
snub you, Kelsey.' He leaned across to close the files on
her desk. 'Come on, I'll take you home. You've been
working too hard recently; you look washed out.' His
voice was gentle and for some unaccountable reason it
made her want to cry.

She made no attempt to argue with him as he took the
pen from her hand and helped her to her feet. He was
right, she had been working too hard. That, plus her
pregnancy and the strain of her marriage, was wearing
her out emotionally as well as physically.

When they got down to the underground car park
Kelsey made to go to her own car, but Brant put a
detaining hand on her shoulder. 'I'll take you home in
my car,' he told her firmly.

She was quite glad to have him drive her home.
Although the snow had been cleared from the main
roads, conditions were still treacherous. She leaned her
head back against the seat and watched Brant's hands on
the steering-wheel, strong and capable.

'How are things going at McConell Real Estate these days?' she asked idly.

'OK,' he answered non-committally.

'Is the new manager that you hired doing a good job?'

'Not bad.' For once Brant didn't seem to want to discuss buisness, so they lapsed into silence, not the uncomfortable silence that had lain between them for weeks—somehow this was different. She closed her eyes, feeling contented for the first time in ages.

When she opened her eyes she experienced a momentary sensation of disorientation. Her head was leaning against something warm and solid and someone was saying her name.

'Kelsey, we're home.' It was Brant's voice and her lips curved in a happy smile.

'Kelsey.' He moved and she realised suddenly that she was leaning against his shoulder and that she must have fallen asleep.

'Sorry.' She straightened slowly, pushing blonde hair back off her face in a sleepy gesture.

'Are you all right?' Dark eyes swept over her pale countenance.

She nodded. 'Just tired.' As his eyes continued to linger on her she put a hand up self-consciously to her tousled hair, unaware of how feminine she looked, or how vulnerable.

'If you want to skip this party tonight and have an early night——'

'No, Brant,' she cut across him. 'I'll be fine once I have a shower. . .honestly.' She added the word firmly, as he looked about to argue.

'OK.' He turned to open the car door. 'Let's just hope our guests don't linger too long.'

The house was a hive of activity. The caterers were putting the finishing touches to the spectacular buffet laid out in the dining-room. Mrs Wright, Brant's housekeeper, was supervising what looked like an army of extra staff. They had festooned the hall and both lounges with glittering Christmas decorations and a large tree stood in one corner, its lights shimmering brightly in the subdue lighting of the room.

Kelsey shook her head in wonder. 'They've done a fabulous job. I can hardly believe it's the same house that we left this morning. I must go and congratulate Mrs Wright.'

'Later.' Brant put a firm hand on her arm. 'If you don't go upstairs and get ready now you won't be down in time to greet your guests.' He gave her a gentle push towards the stairs. 'I'll have a quick word with Mrs Wright.'

As Kelsey stood under the powerful jet of the shower her mind went back over her day's work. She was involved in a bitter custody case between two parents of a five-year-old girl and it was due to come to court in the morning. . .

In the past Kelsey had always tried to distance herself emotionally from the cases that she worked on, otherwise she would have been weighed down by people's problems. She worked hard and conscientiously on each case but at the end of the day when she went home she tried to switch off from them. It was the only way that she could deal with the stress of the job.

In the Woodses' custody case, however, it was different. No matter how hard she tried she couldn't distance herself from the emotionalism that surrounded it.

She sighed as she switched off the shower and reached out for a towel. She could have done without this party this evening; she would have liked to have sat down quietly and studied her notes, ready for tomorrow. Just as you have done for the last week, she told herself wryly. She was being ridiculous; she knew the details of the case backwards. She needed to relax for an evening. Stepping out of the shower, she dried herself and, wrapping a large fluffy towel around her, walked back into the bedroom.

She sat down at her dressing-table and dried her hair

quickly. It was in beautiful condition, and it fell in shining waves around her face. Her skin, however, was a little too pale, making her eyes appear too large for her small, delicate face. Dr Michaels was right, she thought suddenly; she was going to have to start taking things easier. After the Woodses' case she would start cutting her workload a little. She applied a hint of blusher to her cheeks and some pearly lipstick; it made her appear brighter, but she still looked tired.

She put on satin-silk underwear and opened her wardrobe to select the dress that Helen had given to her. She was just fastening the last two buttons at the back when the door opened and Brant walked in.

She smiled shyly over at him. They were together so rarely in the bedroom like this that she felt suddenly very self-conscious. The feeling was made worse by the way his eyes moved slowly over her from the top of her gleaming hair to the slender curves of her body. She felt as if she was burning under that long appraising glance.

'You look like a mermaid in that dress.' He smiled, that attractive slow smile that did very strange things to her heartbeats.

'I'm glad that you like it.' Her voice sounded very prim and proper and as she reached to finish fastening her dress her hands shook slightly as they fumbled with the catches. How was it that Brant could turn her into an awkward adolescent with one sentence, one smile?

He moved over towards her. 'Here, let me.'

She let her hands drop as he went behind her and swiftly fastened the buttons. He didn't move away from her immediately, but stood with his hands resting on her shoulders, his eyes studying their reflection in the mirror opposite. They looked like the perfect couple, Kelsey so delicately feminine next to his strong, rugged good looks. His hands moved from her shoulders to her waist, drawing her back in against him. The dress that she wore shimmered in the lamp light. Blue-green glistening with the silver radiance of mother-of-pearl. His eyes lingered where the dress dipped down between the creamy valley of her breasts.

'Kelsey.' He murmured her name huskily as he bent his head and kissed the satin smooth skin of her shoulders and then the side of her neck.

It was the first time he had touched her in weeks, and she closed her eyes, savouring the ecstasy of the moment.

'On second thoughts maybe I should liken you to a siren.' His deep voice tickled the sensitive skin near her ear and she smiled. 'Enticing me into perilous waters with the sweetness of your smile and the seductive allure of your body.' His lips moved across her high cheek-bones and down towards her lips. She waited for his kiss with a kind of breathless anticipation.

His hands moved from her waist down over the flat plane of her abdomen, resting there in a firm possessive way. That touch sent an electric current of emotion rushing through her and before his lips had closed down on hers she was wrenching herself away from him, her breathing coming in short, shallow gasps.

'Kelsey!' He pulled her around to face him. A frown marred his handsome features. 'What's the matter?'

'Nothing.' She shook her head and tried desperately to get her breathing and her heartbeats back under normal control. 'I'm sorry, Brant, I——'

'You don't have to apologise.' His voice had a deathly quietness about it. The eyes that stared down at her pale countenance were bleak. 'It was my mistake. I seem to make one error after another when it comes to you, Kelsey. But by far the biggest one was accepting the terms of your grandfather's will.'

She flinched at those words and there was raw pain in her eyes as she stared up at him. He turned away from her, raking a hand through thick dark hair. 'You had better go downstairs; our guests will be here in a minute.' He moved towards the bathroom. 'We'll talk later.' The door closed behind him, leaving Kelsey standing where he had left her, feeling totally numb.

She had known for some time that he regretted their marriage, but to hear him say it so coldly after he had been holding her so tenderly was like a raw whiplash across her very soul. She had wanted so much for him to kiss her, to love her.

She closed her eyes and for a moment she could still feel the touch of his hands against her stomach. Possessive and tender, they had been resting over their baby, a baby he knew nothing about. That burning knowledge had been what made her pull away from him. In those few breathless moments she had wanted so much to tell him that she was pregnant, had wanted so much to go into the warm security of his arms and have him tell her that everything would be all right. But of course that had just been another one of her impossible dreams, because things would never be all right, he had just made that perfectly clear.

She could hear the sounds of cars arriving outside. She glanced at herself in the mirror. If she had looked pale before she looked positively ashen now. Taking a deep shaky breath, she went downstairs to face her guests.

Kelsey only had to greet the first couple of guests on her own before Brant came down to stand next to her. He had changed into a dark evening suit and he looked wonderful. Tall, handsome and very distinguished, he stood with one arm resting at her waist and smiled and joked with the steady stream of people who came in through the heavy oak front doors. She couldn't help noticing how the women looked at him as they came in. Some with open adoration, others flirtatious and coy. She tried not to mind and she tried not to notice the envious glances that flickered over her. Little did they know that Brant was just playing the part of her devoted husband, that the arm around her was purely for show and that their marriage was a sham.

Kelsey's worst moment was when Susanna Winters arrived. She waited until she was standing directly in front of Brant before she allowed one of the staff to take

the silver fox coat that was draped dramatically around
her shoulders. She was wearing a white samite dress that
clung to her body, emphasising its slender lines. It was
cut in a Grecian style, covering one shoulder and leaving
the other naked. Kelsey had to admit that it suited her;
it drew attention to the perfect proportions of her figure,
the long length of her neck and delicately shaped face.

'Hello, Kelsey.' Blue eyes moved coolly, almost disdainfully over Kelsey's dress before turning to Brant. It
was hard to tell what she was thinking as she looked up
at him. 'Brant.' Red lips curved into a soft smile and she
reached up to kiss his cheek.

Kelsey looked away and smiled at her escort, a tall
blond man with piercing blue eyes. 'Sorry, Kelsey.'
Susanna turned to introduce them. 'This is Michael
Isaacs, editor of *Modern Woman* magazine.'

Somehow Kelsey managed to shake hands with him
but her smile had become rather fixed. *Modern Woman*
was the magazine that had printed the article about her
marriage to Brant. Now she knew who the reported close
source had been. Susanna had made those hurtful com-
ments about their marriage being a shrewd business
move. Her gaze moved thoughtfully towards the other
woman. Had her words been just a spiteful guess or had
Brant confided in her?

Susanna smiled at her but there was a gleam of
triumph in the cold eyes. Then, linking her arm with
her escort's, she moved away from them to join the
crowds milling through the large house.

'Kelsey.' It was a moment before she realised that
Brant was speaking to her. 'Kelsey, would you like a
drink?'

She looked around and saw that one of the staff was
offering a tray of drinks to her. 'Sorry.' She smiled at
the girl and picked up a crystal glass to nurse it in her
hands. She had stopped drinking since her pregnancy
was confirmed, but, not wanting to draw attention to the
fact, she just held the glass.

'Is something wrong?' Brant enquired lazily.

She glanced up at him in surprise.

'You seemed a little. . .strained around Michael Isaacs.'

Her eyes widened, sometimes Brant could be too perceptive. 'Was it that obvious?' she asked with a grimace.

'Only to me.' He took a sip of his drink. 'Had you met him before?'

She shook her head. 'No, but his magazine ran a feature on us about a week before we married.'

'Did it now?' One dark eyebrow rose. 'Was it any good?'

'Depends on what you think is good,' Kelsey answered drily.

Some more guests arrived to distract their attention and the subject was dropped. For a while after that she was too busy to give much more thought to it as they circulated among their friends and colleagues.

The party was livening up. People were dancing to the pulsating rhythm of a song that was very high in the charts at the moment. Kelsey's eyes flickered over the couples before coming to rest on Susanna and Michael. They were the only ones who weren't moving in time with the beat; their bodies were closely entwined as they moved around slowly as if in a world of their own.

Kelsey moved her attention back to the conversation going on around her and she noticed Brant's attention was also on the dance-floor. His eyes watching Susanna with a far-away expression.

Was he jealous of Michael Isaacs? Her hands clenched into tight fists at her side and her eyes blazed with angry lights. Brant turned at that moment and their eyes met. She severed the connection abruptly, turning to the man who stood beside her to start an animated conversation.

The music changed to a slow romantic beat and out of the corner of her eye she saw Brant going out on to the dance-floor with one of the women from the secretarial pool. He had had quite a few dances with different women but he hadn't once asked her. She turned so that her back was towards them; she didn't want to see Brant with his arms around the slender brunette.

As she moved she caught sight of Daniel across the crowded room and excused herself from the company around her to go over to join him.

'Where have you been until now?' she asked him light-heartedly.

'I'm sorry I'm so late.' He rolled his eyes heavenwards. 'I've had one pig of an evening.'

'Oh?' She slanted him a curious look. 'Come on and I'll get you a drink, and you can tell me all about it.'

'That's the best offer I've had all day.' He grinned.

There was none of Daniel's favourite whiskey out on the bar in the den so they went through to the kitchen to get a new bottle from the cupboard.

'That's better.' Daniel gave a heavy sigh of relief as he poured himself a generous measure and sat down on one of the high kitchen stools. 'Do you mind if we sit in here for a moment? I could do with some peace and quiet.'

'Not at all. It's nice to escape for a while.' She sat on the stool opposite him and poured herself a glass of mineral water. 'Where's your date for this evening?' she asked conversationally. 'It's not like you to come to a party without a beautiful woman on your arm.'

'We've had a quarrel,' Daniel answered glumly.

'Oh, I see.' Kelsey nodded her head sagely, a glimmer of amusement in her eyes. 'So the love bug has finally bitten Daniel Marsden.'

'What makes you say that?' One dark eyebrow rose.

'Because you haven't turned over a few pages of your little black book and brought along a replacement.' She grinned at him.

'But I've had to strike your name out of my little book, Kelsey.' He grinned back at her. 'And you're the only woman I know who compares favourably with Lois.'

'You have got it bad,' Kelsey laughed. She reached up to a cupboard above her head and brought down a jar of peanut butter and some crackers which she proceeded to spread liberally as she spoke. 'I knew there was someone serious in your life when you bought Joe's house.' She pushed the plate towards him, but he shook his head and poured himself another whiskey instead.

'I prefer to call it temporary insanity,' he said gloomily. 'But lord, she is beautiful.'

Kelsey smiled. 'So what happened?'

'She wants to settle down, house in the country, roses around the door, that sort of thing.'

'So you bought Joe's house and decided to settle down with her?'

'Something like that.' He leaned his head in his hands and for a moment his handsome features were overcast with misery. 'I bought the house as a surprise for her, told her we could get a team of interior decorators and do whatever she wanted to it. I thought she would be thrilled.'

'Didn't she like it?' Kelsey frowned. The house was very beautiful, but then not everyone's taste was the same.

'She likes it all right, she just wouldn't live in it with me.'

'Oh, I see. . .' Kelsey was silent for a moment, her green eyes sympathetic as they studied him. She knew what he was going through. Unrequited love was a very painful experience. 'It's better that you find out now that she doesn't love you before you get in any deeper,' she told him gently.

He frowned at her. 'No, Kelsey, you don't understand. She loves me all right, she's just not prepared to live with me. She wants marriage, children, the whole works.' Dark blue eyes narrowed on her. 'Do you know, she even had the nerve to tell me to sell my pad in town?'

'Oh!' Kelsey tried hard to smother the laughter that

bubbled up inside her, but with little avail. 'That's dreadful, Daniel! Some women have no consideration.'

'This isn't funny, Kel.' He shook his head. 'She's backed me into a corner.'

'Well, let's face it Daniel, it had to happen sooner or later.' She grinned at him. 'I hope you are going to send me a wedding invitation.'

'Who said I was going to marry the woman?' He looked completely horrified.

'You don't have to say it. Look at you, Daniel, you're totally miserable without her. You're not interested in other women, you couldn't even raise the enthusiasm to bring another date with you this evening.' Kelsey shook her head in a mock-solemn way. 'I don't think that bachelor-pad in town is going to be of any use to you any more.'

'Good grief, you certainly know how to depress a guy!' Daniel muttered, but there was a gleam of humour in his blue eyes now. 'Looks like I'm doomed to a life of domesticity. Unless I can persuade you to leave your husband and run away with me?'

'It's a tempting offer, Daniel.' Her eyes sparkled with humour for a moment before growing suddenly serious. 'But I think Brant's stuck with me for a little while longer. Duty bound for better or for worse.' She gave him a sad smile.

'Kelsey.' Daniel reached across to take her hand, but she never did hear what he was going to say because a deep voice interrupted them from behind, making them both jump.

'I hate to intrude on such a cosy scene.' Brant was standing just inside the kitchen door. His manner was relaxed, yet that was curiously at odds with the cold expression in the dark eyes that swept over them.

'Brant!' Daniel was the first to recover his equilibrium. 'I'm afraid I have been monopolising your wife. She's been advising me on a small problem of mine.'

'Really?' One dark eyebrow rose drily. 'Maybe in future you would be better writing to "Dear Abby".'

Daniel gave a small nervous laugh. 'You could be right. Why don't you come and join us, Brant? Help me kill this bottle of whiskey.'

'No, thanks.' Brant's eyes swept over to Kelsey. 'I only came to ask my wife if she would have a courtesy dance with me. I think people will expect to see us together at least once out there.'

And we must keep up appearances, Kelsey thought bitterly. She shrugged slim shoulders. 'I'll be out in a moment,' she told him coolly.

There was a brief flicker of anger in the dark eyes, then abruptly he turned and left them.

'Phew!' Daniel let his breath escape in a long sigh of relief. 'I wonder how much of our conversation he overheard?'

Kelsey shook her head. 'I don't know, I didn't hear him come in.'

'Oh, no, I hope he didn't hear me joking about your leaving him. I'd hate him to get the wrong idea. I happen to like my job with Harcourt McConell.'

'Don't be silly, Daniel, Brant's not like that,' Kelsey assured him quickly. She forbore to tell him that Brant had already got the wrong idea about them and that he didn't give a damn. 'He's a little annoyed because I've neglected my duties as hostess for too long, nothing more than that.' She got to her feet with a sigh. 'Come on, I suppose we'll have to go and circulate.'

The party seemed to be going very well; everyone looked as if they were having a good time. Daniel paused by the door leading through to the dining-room. 'I think I'll go and help myself to some of that delicious-looking food from your buffet.' He smiled at her. 'Can I get you something, smoked salmon and a little caviar?'

She grimaced at the very thought. 'No thanks, I think I'll just go and find Brant.'

'OK, see you later.'

She had no difficulty in finding her husband. He was on the dance-floor, his arms around Susanna as they danced to a slow, romantic ballad.

Kelsey stood and watched them with a kind of numb coldness surrounding her heart. Susanna's back was towards her, her arms raised around Brant's neck, while his hands were resting out flat, one on her bare shoulder, the other at the slender curve of her hip. Dark hair was bent close to her short blonde hair as he spoke in a low voice next to her ear. When he finally raised his head, Kelsey found herself looking directly into his eyes.

The dark gaze was inscrutable. It locked on her and seemed to burn into her very soul as if searching for something he needed to see. She swallowed down the bitter emotions that rose inside her and returned his gaze with as much indifference as she could muster. It was only when he returned his attention to the woman in his arms that she was able to drag herself away, feeling sick to her very heart.

She never did dance with Brant, for the simple reason that he never came over to ask her. He danced with a long succession of other women, though. Every time she saw him there was a beautiful woman clinging to his arm, smiling up at him. Kelsey swallowed down the hurt inside and somehow managed to carry on conversations and laugh at people's jokes as if there was nothing amiss.

By the time most of their guests had left, Kelsey was feeling emotionally and physically exhausted. She moved through to the dining-room and started to help the staff clear away the food that had been left.

Mrs Wright looked horrified when she walked into the kitchen a while later to find Kelsey reloading the dish-washer. 'Mrs Harcourt! What on earth are you doing?' She rushed to take the pile of crockery from her. 'I've more than enough staff to help me do this.'

'Yes, I know, but as it's so late I thought I'd lend a hand.'

'That's not necessary,' the housekeeper assured her

firmly. Her eyes moved over Kelsey's pale complexion. 'Why don't you go on up to bed? You're looking a little tired.'

Kelsey smiled at the understatement. 'I'd like to, but there are still a few guests drinking in the den. I thought it might be a bit rude just to leave them.'

Mrs Wright shook her head. 'You run along. Mr Harcourt is in there with them. I'm sure they won't even notice you've gone.'

'Probably not,' Kelsey agreed wryly, and then smiled as she had to stifle a yawn. 'You're right, I am exhausted. I think I will turn in.'

It was such a relief to get into the sanctuary of her bedroom. She had overdone things today, and her whole body seemed to ache with sheer fatigue.

She kicked off her shoes and unbuttoned her dress, allowing it to slither to the floor. Then she lay down on top of the bed-covers in her camisole and silk pants. She only meant to lie there for a moment, just until she had the energy to change into her nightdress. One minute she was staring open-eyed at the ceiling of her room, the next she was fast asleep.

'Kelsey.' Brant's voice penetrated the mists of sleep that surrounded her. 'Kelsey, wake up. I want to come to bed.'

She sighed heavily and stretched. Her movements were languorous and unconsciously provocative. 'What time is it?' she murmured sleepily, lifting a hand to shield her eyes from the bright overhead light.

'Late.' He switched the light off and flicked on the softer bedside lamp. He took off his jacket and put it down on the chair beside him, then he loosened his tie. As he undressed his eyes moved over the slender length of Kelsey's body. The long smooth legs, the soft curve of her hips, the gentle swell of her breasts under the satin-silk camisole, the tumbled disorder of her blonde hair against the darker covers of the bed. 'Are you going to move over to your side of the bed?' His voice had a harsh rasping edge to it.

'What?' Hazily she sat up a little and realised that she was lying sideways across the bed, stopping him from getting in. 'Sorry.' She was aware that he was watching her but she was too tired to feel self-conscious as she slid over to her own side of the bed. As she moved, the fragile straps of her camisole slipped down to reveal the creamy curve of her breast. Slowly she adjusted the silk so that she was covered again, then leaned her head back against the pillows, wishing that she had the energy to crawl beneath the covers.

'Are you deliberately trying to provoke me, Kelsey?' His voice had an ominous ring to it that made her glance quickly up at him.

His broad chest was bare and he was unfastening the belt on his trousers, but it was the expression in his eyes that caught and held her attention. They were glittering brilliantly with something that Kelsey dimly recognised through the sleepy haze that surrounded her as intense male desire.

'No. . .no, of course not.' She moved nervously. She had been longing for weeks for him to look at her like that. But there was something intense and frightening about his mood; it was as if there were a million angry emotions just barely held in check within that powerful body.

'No?' One dark eyebrow rose mockingly. 'I think you are, Kelsey, I think you want me to finish what Marsden started tonight.'

'I don't know what you're talking about.' She shook her head helplessly, she was too tired to be able to concentrate on what he was saying.

'I'm talking about the way Marsden was coming on to you this evening in that blatantly sexual approach,' he grated harshly.

'There was nothing sexual, we were just talking——'

'And he just happened to drop in the fact that he

would like you to leave me and go away with him?' he
cut across her, his voice harshly derisive.

'You're taking it all out of context.' She rolled on to
her side so that her back was towards him. 'Please,
Brant, let's not argue,' she whispered miserably. 'I can't
stand it, I feel awful.'

There was a moment's silence, then she felt his hand
on her arm. 'Well, let's see if I can make you feel better,
shall we?'

He pulled her around to face him. For a moment she
stared up at him wide-eyed. His dark eyes held hers and
she drew in a sharp breath at the look she saw there; a
bitter, haunted expression that scared her, yet somehow
held her captive at the same time.

Slowly he lowered his head, and she closed her eyes as
his lips touched hers. They moved gently over her mouth
at first; she could taste the faint traces of whiskey that he
had been drinking, smell the clean fragrance of his skin
and his hair. She returned his kiss, gently, hesitantly, a
wealth of feeling in the softness of her lips. He pulled
away from her a little and his eyes moved down over her
body in a blatant, sensual appraisal. His hands touched
her breasts through the silk of her underwear, shaping
their rounded curves through the softness of the
material. Then he pulled the camisole down and his
hands moved over her skin in a slow, deliberate caress.

She drew in a long shuddering breath as his lips moved
down towards her and for the first time she touched him.
Her fingers brushed through the thick darkness of his
hair and slid down to his shoulders, her nails pressing
into his skin as she felt the pressure of his mouth against
her breasts.

Then he simply lost control.

CHAPTER TEN

Dawn had broken when Kelsey woke up. A narrow shaft of wintry sunlight filtered through the curtains at the far end of the room. It cast a golden trail of light across the peach carpet and highlighted the peach-gold satin bedclothes that partially covered her and Brant.

He was lying on his side, facing her, still deeply asleep, one arm stretched out across her waist. She turned towards him and his arm curved instinctively around her, the palm of his hand pressed against the bare skin of her back.

In sleep his powerful features were strangely vulnerable. She reached out a hand contemplatively to touch the strong muscles of his upper arm. She liked the feel of his firm smooth skin and ran her fingers in a light caressing movement up on to his broad shoulders. He was sleeping deeply, the forceful strength of his body relaxed after a night of intense lovemaking.

Memories from the night flooded through her mind. He had taken her again and again, almost as if he couldn't get enough of her, and his manner had been none too gentle. She hadn't tried to resist him; even if she had wanted to she had known that any struggles would be ineffectual and useless. He had shown her no tenderness, had spoken no words of love, but she had loved him with a bitter-sweet depth of emotion that somehow had managed to cancel out the pain she had felt.

A lock of dark hair had fallen on to his forehead and she pushed it back with gentle fingers. Her eyes watched him with a kind of hungry intensity as he slept. It was lovely being able to study him so openly with no fears of being caught and made to feel foolish. Her fingers traced the straight dark line of his eyebrow. Even in sleep he had beautiful eyes, the long dark lashes resting against bronzed skin. Her fingers trailed down the side of his face and her attention moved to his mouth, firm and sensual in spite of the sleep that claimed him. Impulsively she leaned towards him and touched her lips to his in a feather-light caress. For a moment she allowed herself to dream that Brant was in love with her. It was a wonderful fantasy and it felt almost real lying here in the strong circle of his arms. But of course it wasn't; she forced the illusion away, suddenly angry with herself. Hadn't she learnt her lesson yet? How many times did Brant have to hurt her before it was brought home to her how unlikely that possibility was? Dreaming unrealistic dreams was only going to leave her wide open to more disillusionment and pain. Brant didn't love her and he would never love her; the sooner she came to terms with that the better.

Very carefully she extricated herself from Brant's arms and climbed quietly out of bed. He rolled over on to his back but he didn't waken, much to her relief. She glanced at her watch; it was nearly seven, very soon the alarm clock would be going off. She picked up her underwear and her dress from the floor; as she straightened the familiar nausea began to gnaw at the pit of her stomach. She tried very hard to fight it down but it was no good. Dropping her clothes, she rushed towards the bathroom.

It was the worst bout of sickness that she had had in a long time. When it finally abated she felt completely drained and all she felt like doing was climbing back into bed. She rinsed her face, being careful not to look at her chalk-white reflection in the mirror above the basin. She reached for a large bath towel and wrapped it around her, then she sat on the bathroom floor and waited for the next attack, which she knew from experience would follow quickly.

That was where Brant found her, on the floor, huddled

in a white bath towel, her head buried down between her knees so that all he could see was the top of her ruffled blonde hair.

'Kelsey?' The deep masculine voice made her lift her head and look up at him.

He was standing in the doorway wearing a white towelling robe, an expression of shock in his dark eyes.

She buried her head down again. No wonder he looked shocked, she thought miserably; she was a complete mess. Her pale face was streaked with tears, her hair was in wild disorder.

'Kelsey, what is it? What's the matter?' He knelt down beside her and she felt his hand gently smoothing back her hair.

'Nothing.' Her voice was thick and muffled. 'Please go away, Brant, I don't want you here.' She felt nausea gripping her stomach painfully. She didn't want him to see her being sick, and she didn't want him to see her in this state. 'Go away.' She put out her arms to push him away but somehow she felt herself drawn in against him and held in the warm circle of his arms. Her first reaction was to struggle away from him, but his hand was rubbing her back in such a soothing way that she found herself relaxing against him. He murmured deep calming words against her ear and she curled her arms up and around his neck.

After a while her breathing steadied and the nausea started to melt away. He picked her up gently and carried her back into the bedroom to lay her with infinite care down on to the bed.

She kept her eyes closed for a moment and felt the bed give under his weight as he sat down beside her. 'Better now?'

She nodded, but still didn't open her eyes. He stroked her hair gently back off her face and then his fingers moved down to her shoulder and the top of her arm. She winced at the unexpected pain she felt there and her eyes flew open.

A dark ugly bruise marked the top of her arm. It must have been from the way Brant had held her last night, although she hadn't felt him hurting her like that.

'Oh, Kelsey, I'm sorry, I never meant to hurt you.' His voice was bitter with self-recrimination, and her eyes moved with surprise towards his face.

'You didn't.' She smiled gently up at him. 'I've always bruised easily.'

He shook his head. 'I don't deserve for you to forgive me so easily. Not after what happened in there.' He indicated the bathroom with a flick of his hand.

She frowned, not understanding what he meant.

'I behaved brutishly.' He raked an angry hand through his hair. 'My only defence is that I had too much to drink and I was. . .' He trailed off abruptly. 'But there's really no excuse for that kind of conduct.'

It suddenly dawned on her that Brant was blaming his behaviour last night for the way she had been so violently sick this morning. She opened her mouth to assure him that it was not like that, then closed it again. If she told him that, then she would have to tell him the real reason for her sickness. Indecision tore at her—was this the right time to tell him?

The shrill ringing of the alarm clock took the onus away from her. Brant leaned across and switched it off. 'We can't go on like this, Kelsey,' he murmured. He got to his feet, looking suddenly tired. 'When I get home tonight we will have to sit down and talk.'

'Yes,' she answered him quietly and her heart started to beat loudly with apprehension. She had been wanting to sit down and talk with him for weeks, but hearing him say it like that gave her the awful feeling that she wasn't going to like what he would say to her.

He moved towards the wardrobe to take out his clothes and she started to swing her legs down from the bed.

'What are you doing?' He turned back to her with a frown.

Getting ready for work,' she answered simply. 'I have
the Woodses court case today.'

'Oh, no, you don't. You're not well enough to work
today.'

'But Brant, I——'

'The subject is not open for discussion,' he interrupted
her firmly. 'The trial will just have to be postponed to a
later date.' He took a dark grey suit out of his wardrobe
and disappeared into the bathroom to turn the shower
on. As far as he was concerned the matter ended there.

But Kelsey had other ideas on the subject. She
couldn't let the Woodses' case be postponed; it wasn't
fair to Anita Woods. The poor woman had worked
herself up into a highly emotional state ready for the
hearing this morning; she couldn't in all conscience ring
her and tell her it had been deferred to another date. . .
Resolutely she swung her legs off the bed and went to
the wardrobe to select a plain black suit before heading
down the corridor towards one of the other bathrooms.

She was in the kitchen making toast and coffee when
he came downstairs. 'I thought if I made your breakfast
you might feel more inclined towards giving me a ride
into the office.'

The note of levity fell on deaf ears; he was not amused.
Dark eyes swept over her slender figure in the tailored
business suit, then moved to where her briefcase was
sitting next to the door, ready just to be picked up on
the way out. 'When I told you not to come into work
today I was speaking as your boss, not your husband,'
he told her drily.

'Really?' A glint of anger flared briefly in her green
eyes. 'Well, if my boss has something to say to me he
should send me a memo at the office. I don't take orders
in the bedroom.'

Firm lips twisted into a half-smile. 'Now, that is a
pity,' he drawled lazily.

Bright colour lit her cheeks at those words, at the way
he said them. She turned to pour him some coffee,

irritated with herself for allowing him to fluster her so easily.

'I know the case I'm working on is inconsequential compared to the one you are involved in, Brant, but it's important to me and it's important to Anita Woods.' She passed his drink over to him. 'If you don't give me a lift into work I'll take a cab,' she told him firmly.

One dark eyebrow rose. Very few people ever dared to flout Brant's authority. For a moment Kelsey held her breath, wondering if she had gone too far.

'You are one hell of a stubborn woman.' he smiled crookedly. 'Makes me wonder how I managed to talk you into marrying me.'

She relaxed, knowing that he had relented, and smiled back. 'You are a defence lawyer who happens to be very good at breaking down people's defences,' she told him lightly.

'Good, but not nearly good enough,' he murmured, and there was a bitter note of irony in his voice that Kelsey did not understand. He glanced at his watch. 'Time we were going.'

Kelsey nodded and moved to pick up her briefcase.

They travelled into the office in total silence. Brant seemed deep in thought, his manner self-contained and aloof. His mind was probably centred very firmly on the day's work that lay ahead of him, Kelsey guessed as she shot a glance at his stern profile. She wished that she had his ability to shut everything out of his mind except work. She wished that she could forget the way he had set her body on fire last night, the way he had made her feel.

When they pulled into Brant's space in the car park Daniel was just getting out of his car, and he stood and waited for them at the doors to the lift.

'Just wanted to thank you both for such a lovely party last night.' His smile encompassed them both and then lingered on the pallor of Kelsey's skin. 'You don't look very well this morning, Kel; are you all right?'

She nodded. 'A bit of a hangover, that's all,' she murmured dismissively.

'First time that I ever heard of someone having a hangover from drinking mineral water.' Daniel grinned.

Thankfully Kelsey was saved from having to make a reply to that by the lift doors opening behind them.

'How's the Sharman trial progressing, Brant?' Daniel asked in a jovial tone as they walked in. 'You've sure been hitting the headlines with it.'

'I suppose that depends on what kind of newspapers you read,' Brant answered drily. He reached and pressed the buttons on the wall panel, floor twenty for the other two, and the top one for himself.

There was silence for a while as the lift slid smoothly upwards.

'I've got the decorators coming over to look round the house today, Kel.' Daniel smiled over at her. 'If you have time I'd appreciate having a chat with you about it. I could do with some pointers before I talk to them.'

Before Kelsey had a chance to answer, Brant cut into the conversation. 'I hardly think you need Kelsey's help to redecorate your apartment.'

Daniel shook his head. 'No, you misunderstand me, Brant. I'm talking about Joe's old house, or rather my new house.' Incisive blue eyes turned towards Kelsey. 'You are right about the apartment, Kel, I thought it over last night. I don't need or want a bachelor-pad any longer.'

His voice was so momentous that Kelsey had to smile. She flicked a glance over at Brant and the smile rapidly faded as she met the full force of his glittering, cold gaze.

'So how about it, Kel? Are you free for lunch today so I can run a few ideas by you?' Daniel reclaimed her attention.

'Well, I'm in court today,' she murmured.

The doors swished open on the twentieth floor and Daniel took her arm as they left. 'Well, perhaps we can arrange something a little later?'

'I don't know, Daniel.' Kelsey cast a backwards glance at Brant but the doors were already closing behind them as the lift continued up to the top floor. 'I think you should be consulting your girlfriend about the décor of your house, not me.'

'Yes, I know.' Daniel sighed heavily. 'But she's still not talking to me. I rang her this morning at a very early hour when I knew she would be there. All I got was the answering machine.'

'Well, perhaps she was still asleep,' Kelsey suggested logically.

'No, she's not talking to me.' They stopped outside their respective offices. 'But I intend to rectify the situation this evening.' He gave her a supremely confident smile and she had to laugh.

'I wish you luck. In the meantime ring your decorators and postpone them until you've sorted everything out.'

'Yes, I suppose you're right.' Daniel paused with his hand on his office door. 'By the way, Kel, you did tell Brant that I had bought Joe's house, didn't you?'

'I can't remember if I did or not.' She shrugged lightly. 'We've both been so busy lately.' Noticing that her secretary was signalling to her through the glass doors, she moved away from him. 'I'll have to go, Daniel. Speak to you later.'

'Calvin Davis, Mr Woods's attorney, on line one,' Maggie informed her immediately as she walked in.

'Thanks.' Kelsey headed into her office and picked up the phone. 'Kelsey Harcourt speaking,' she said in crisply decisive tones. From them on there was no time to think of anything except the day's workload.

There were very few people in the courtroom, just Kelsey's client and across from them the woman's ex-husband and his lawyer and then a handful of people who were to appear as witnesses. For a moment Kelsey couldn't help comparing it with the Sharman trial, which was being held in the same building. She had caught a glimpse of the crowds waiting to enter that courtroom as she had arrived, and her first thought had been for Brant. The stress of handling a case of that size must be enormous.

The judge entered the court and everyone rose to their feet. Kelsey firmly pushed all thoughts of Brant from her mind as she prepared for the ordeal ahead. She had been disappointed in the judge who was to hear the case. She had hoped for a woman, but instead they had got Judge Robinson, a man who was not noted for his compassion. Bearing in mind that he was not going to be influenced or directed by emotional pleas, Kelsey had prepared her case accordingly.

As she got to her feet to make her opening address she gave a reassuring smile to her client, who was looking pale and drawn. Then she started to speak, her voice crisp and confident. Kelsey was good at her job and it shone through in her words and in her manner. She looked like a woman who was very much in control of the situation.

The door into the courtroom opened and someone came in. Kelsey didn't look around. Her hair gleamed like polished gold as she bent her head to briefly consult her notes.

'Mr Woods's accusations that his wife is an unfit mother are completely unfounded. Before we put Mrs Woods on the stand there are a number of witnesses I would like to call.'

The case was emotionally charged and very heavy going. It took every ounce of Kelsey's expertise and concentration to get through the next few hours. Her client's ex-husband was obviously prepared to go to any lengths to get his daughter back and things started to get very distressing for Anita Woods.

It was at this point that the judge called a recess until after the weekend, when he expressed a wish to see the child in question in his chambers.

'Why does he want to see Eleanor?' Anita asked Kelsey

as people started to file out of the court. 'She's only a baby.'

Kelsey closed her briefcase and turned to reassure her client. 'It's just a formality, don't worry about it. The judge probably just wants to satisfy himself that the child looks as if she is being well cared for and that she seems well adjusted—that kind of thing.'

A hand touched her arm and she turned to find Brant standing next to her. She was so taken aback by his presence that for a moment she couldn't find her voice. 'Brant, this is a surprise,' she murmured finally. Just looking up at that ruggedly attractive face made her heartbeats increase dramatically. What on earth was he doing in here? she wondered.

Aware that Anita was still waiting anxiously to have a word with her, Kelsey turned and introduced the woman to her husband.

'Mr Harcourt.' Anita rose quickly to her feet and shook hands with Brant. Then she turned worried eyes back on Kelsey. 'Things didn't go all that well today, did they?'

'I warned you that it would be tough, Anita,' Kelsey told her gently. 'But I don't think it went too badly. I'm quietly confident.'

'You have an excellent attorney, Mrs Woods,' Brant put in, his voice calm and reassuring. 'That is half the battle.'

'Yes.' The woman suddenly looked a little happier and she smiled at Kelsey. 'I'll see you on Monday morning, then?'

Kelsey nodded and watched as the woman left them. When the door closed behind her she was left alone in the courtroom with Brant.

'Thanks for the vote of confidence just now.' She slanted a look up at him and found he was watching her with a curious expression on his hard features.

'I meant every word,' he replied seriously. 'I've been

listening in for the last couple of hours and I was very impressed by you.'

'Were you?' Her voice had a slight huskiness which she fought hard to eliminate. His praise meant so much to her. 'So, why aren't you in court doing battle with the Sharman trial?' She changed the subject with a lightness of tone which she was far from feeling. She had an awful sense of foreboding at seeing him here like this.

'Because it finished almost before it got going this morning. I decided it had dragged on long enough.'

Her eyes widened. 'You won the case?'

'Well, of course I won!' His lips curved in a brief arrogant smile.

'Oh, Brant, that's wonderful!' For a moment she almost forgot herself and flung herself into his arms. She stopped herself just in time. 'I'm so pleased for you,' she murmured instead.

'Thanks.' There was a grim note to his voice that she didn't understand.

There was a moment of strained silence. Then he raked a hand in a weary gesture through thick dark hair. 'I was going to wait until this evening to talk to you but now that the Sharman trial has finished I've booked myself on this afternoon's flight to Vancouver. The conference that I'm to attend doesn't start for another couple of days but I may as well leave early; it will give me a chance to rest for a few days at the hotel before it starts.'

'I see,' Kelsey answered quietly. She knew very well that Brant was leaving early because he wanted to put some distance between them. He was tired of her and tired of their marriage.

'God, Kelsey, this is the hardest thing I've ever had to say,' he rasped suddenly.

She looked hurriedly away from him. Then don't say it, she wanted to scream. She was suddenly filled with the urge to cover her ears and refuse to listen, like some child who was afraid to face up to the truth.

'It doesn't take a genius to work out that our marriage is failing.' He paused for a moment, as if waiting for her to say something. She remained silent, staring down at the floor. Her heart was thumping so loudly that it was painful.

'I never meant to make you unhappy, Kelsey, please believe that. I truly did believe that we could make a go of things. It's patently obvious to me now that I was very, very wrong.'

A terrible weakness assailed her at those words and she had to swallow hard to retain her composure.

'What I'm trying to say, Kelsey, is that if you want your freedom, then file for a divorce now. I won't stand in your way.'

'What about the McConell shares?' Her voice was little more than a whisper and she still couldn't look up at him.

'They have ceased to matter to me.' His mouth twisted in a bitter smile as he noticed how that made her head jerk up. 'That discovery came as quite a surprise to me too. It hit me out of the blue and I suddenly realised how wrong I've been about everything. You can't build a marriage on business contracts or even physical desire. There has got to be love; without it no relationship stands a chance of surviving.'

'You've fallen in love,' she murmured, a note of numb incredulity in her voice.

'Hard to believe, isn't it?' he said derisively.

Kelsey didn't find it hard to believe at all. Not when she thought about the way Brant had held Susanna on the dance-floor last night. Seeing her with another man must have made him realise how much he loved her. Probably when they had made love last night Brant had wished it was Susanna lying in his arms.

'So when do you think I should move out?' Was that her voice, so calm and cool?

'I don't want you to rush into anything, Kelsey; take your time and think what will be the best thing for you,' he told her gently. 'I realise I pressurised you into marrying me and I don't want to push you now into something you'll regret. More than anything else I want you to be happy.'

'That's very noble of you,' she murmured, a bitter edge to her voice.

'Don't worry about your position in the McConell company. I'll make sure that you are financially secure,' Brant told her firmly.

Kelsey didn't say anything—she felt too numb. The last thing in the world that she cared about was the business or finances.

Brant stretched out a hand and for a moment she thought he was going to touch her. She moved a step back from him; she couldn't bear for him to come anywhere near her. If he did she knew that she would just break down and cry.

His hand dropped back down by his side. 'Think things over, Kelsey,' he told her quietly. 'We'll talk when I get back.'

Then he left her alone in the courtroom. A fitting place for their marriage to end, Kelsey thought with heart-rending bitterness.

The house didn't feel like a home, not without Brant. After the weekend Kelsey felt as if she was going to go crazy. She had hardly slept for two nights. Her mind was on overdrive wondering where Brant was staying, whom he was staying with. Had Susanna gone to Vancouver with him? She imagined them together and Brant saying the words to Susanna that she had longed to hear him say to herself—that he loved her.

On Sunday night Kelsey packed her car with some of her clothes and possessions and drove back to her flat in town. At least there she wouldn't be plagued with waiting for the phone to ring.

It was ridiculous to hope that Brant might phone. Your husband didn't tell you that he wanted a divorce, go away with another woman, and then ring to ask if you were all right.

Her flat was cold and damp, even though she had set the heating on a timer to come on once a day. It also looked bare without her pictures and books; it made her feel even more miserable just looking around.

At nine that evening she went upstairs and made up her bed with fresh laundry. On the floor next to her bed she found the copy of *Modern Woman* magazine that she had left there just before her wedding. That was when she sat down and cried for the first time since Brant had left her.

On Monday morning it was snowing heavily again and the temperature had plunged to an all-time low. Kelsey shivered as she got out of bed. The apartment was freezing; it felt as if the heating wasn't working. She struggled into a dressing-gown and hurried downstairs to look. As she had suspected, the heating system had failed to come on and, no matter how many times she flicked the switches, it refused to start.

By the time she had rung the heating engineers and left a key with her next door neighbours she was late starting out to work.

She had meant to ring through to Susanna Winters's office when she got in, just to find out where she was, but there was no time for that. She had to go directly to the courts. She had told Anita Woods that she would see her outside the judge's chambers at ten. It was nearly ten-past when she finally arrived.

She need not have hurried, however, because the judge kept them waiting for nearly half an hour. As they sat in the corridor outside the chambers Kelsey watched little Eleanor Woods playing with her doll. The child looked cute in a red tartan skirt, red tights and jumper. Her blonde hair was in tight curls. Kelsey's heart went out to her. It was so tragic when a marriage went wrong, especially when there were children involved. No matter which one of the child's parents won custody, all of them

would lose. No one won in a situation like this. Her
mind turned towards her own problems. At least she
would never have to go through a custody case, she
thought grimly. Brant didn't want her and he certainly
wouldn't want his child.

The door at the far end of the corridor opened and
Anita's ex-husband walked in. At first the little girl
didn't notice her father, then, when she did, her doll
was forgotten and she ran over to him to be swung up
into his arms.

He walked over towards them with the child and, with
a brief nod at Kelsey, spoke to his wife. 'Anita, do you
think I could speak to you outside?'

Anita Woods hesitated for a moment and then shook
her head.

He put down the child and crouched down beside his
ex-wife's chair. 'I just wanted to tell you I'm sorry about
the way things went in court on Friday. I never meant
for my attorney to say those things about you.'

Kelsey shifted uncomfortably in her chair, wondering
if she should try to put a stop to this conversation.

'Anita, please talk to me before we go any further with
this custody thing.'

Kelsey looked over at him to interrupt and then
stopped herself as she noticed the tears that shone in the
man's eyes. 'Anita, would you like me to leave you alone
for a little while?' she asked instead.

There was a brief silence and then the woman nodded.
Kelsey went back out into the main corridors. She was
standing by the vending machine, waiting for a cup of
coffee that she didn't really want, when a man's voice
called out her name.

'Hello, Daniel.' She smiled at him, then turned to
pick up her coffee. 'How's the love-life?'

'Couldn't be better.' He grinned at her. 'We've set the
date.'

'Congratulations.' Kelsey leaned over to kiss his
cheek. 'I hope you won't forget my invitation?'

'You're top of our list.' Daniel smiled and then became serious suddenly. 'What I really came over to tell you was that I got the strangest phone call last night from Brant.'

'Oh?' Kelsey frowned. 'Why was he phoning you?'

'That's what I can't work out. He said he'd been trying to phone you all night at home and he thought for some reason that you would be with me. He more or less demanded to speak to you. Didn't seem to believe me when I told him you weren't with me.' Daniel shrugged. 'For one awful moment I wondered if he thought there was something going on between us. . .' He trailed off, looking suddenly embarrassed. 'Anyway, just in case he did, I told him all about Lois and our engagement. To say the guy was stunned is putting it mildly.'

'Well, I think we're all pretty stunned. Nobody ever had you pegged as the serious type.' Kelsey tried to make light of the situation. Brant had probably been annoyed to find that she wasn't with Daniel; it would have salved his conscience to think they were having an affair.

'I tried to phone you after he'd rung off, but there was no answer from your house.'

'No. . . I was at my apartment last night,' Kelsey told him reluctantly. She didn't want to go into details; she didn't want people to know yet about her marriage breaking up. Luckily she didn't have to explain any further because a sudden commotion at the far end of the corridor diverted Daniel's attention.

'My case is being called into court,' he turned back to her with a rueful smile. 'I'll have to go, Kel—speak to you later.'

When Kelsey went back to join her client she found Anita Woods in a tight embrace with her husband. Eleanor came running over to her, blue eyes shining with excitement. 'Daddy is going to come home with us,' she informed Kelsey.

'Is he?' Kelsey crouched down beside the little girl

and ruffled her blonde curls. 'Well, I'm very glad to hear it.'

With the Woodses' case coming to an abrupt end, Kelsey was able to take an earlier appointment at her doctor's that afternoon. She wasn't surprised when he told her that her blood-pressure was up a little.

'You'll have to start taking things a bit easier, Kelsey,' Dr Michaels told her seriously. 'Start resting more, otherwise we will be taking you in for an enforced rest.'

Taking his words to heart, Kelsey didn't go back into the office but went to her flat, stopping briefly to pick up some groceries. It felt almost like old times, balancing brown paper bags as she struggled to get the front door open.

'Here, let me help.' The deep, familiar voice made Kelsey's heart miss several beats.

She turned and her eyes locked hungrily on her husband's ruggedly handsome face. The dark overcoat that he wore emphasised his broad shoulders and added to that aura of power that always surrounded him. The dark eyes that gazed down at her were strangely intense.

'What are you doing here, Brant?' She finally found her voice.

'I was going to ask you the same question.' He reached to take the heavy bags from her. 'Well, are we going to stand out here until it gets dark or are you going to open the door?'

Her hands trembled slightly as she turned to put the key in the lock.

Thankfully the apartment was warm; her heating system had obviously been fixed. Kelsey led the way through to the kitchen and waited while Brant put the groceries down on top of one of the counters.'

'Has your conference finished?' she asked, puzzled by his presence.

'No, it hasn't started yet.' He turned to look at her. She had taken off her coat and she stood next to the table looking slim and very beautiful in a red cashmere dress. 'I came back because I was worried about you.'

Anger flared in her green eyes. She didn't want him to worry or to feel sorry for her. 'Well, you needn't have bothered. I'm perfectly all right and I'm well able to manage on my own.'

'Yes, I suppose you are.' His mouth twisted as if he didn't like that thought very much. 'I tried to ring you at home last night.'

'I was here. This is my home now.' There was an uncomfortable silence. Kelsey moved to start putting the groceries away, afraid that if she didn't keep busy she might do something foolish like run into his arms and beg him to take her back.

'I rang Daniel last night. He told me that he is engaged to a woman called Lois Thorpe.'

'I know.' Kelsey banged cupboard doors open and closed with unnecessary force.

'Are you upset about it?' he asked quietly.

'Why should I be upset?' Blonde hair swung angrily round as she glared at him. 'Daniel and I have only ever been good friends.'

Silence met that statement. Kelsey turned to put the last bag of sugar into the cupboard above her head. 'If you've come rushing back here out of some kind of guilt, because you don't want to think of my being on my own, then you needn't have bothered. I was perfectly happy living on my own for years and I will be perfectly happy again. You are wasting your time feeling sorry or guilty about me.'

'But that's just it, Kelsey.' His voice was low and steady. 'You may be able to take up from where you left off but I won't. I don't want to go back to living without you.'

The sugar dropped from her fingers and hit the floor with a force that burst the bag and sent sugar flying everywhere. Green eyes glimmered with tears as she stared over at him. 'I don't know what kind of game you're playing now, Brant, but it's not fair. It's cruel coming here saying things like that.' She bent to start clearing up the mess and as she did a horrid shaft of weakness seemed to sweep over her. She clutched at the worktop, one hand going instinctively and protectively to her stomach.

'Kelsey, what is it?' He was beside her in a minute. Strong arms moved around her and he was swinging her up into his arms to carry her back into the lounge. It felt so lovely to be back in his arms again. For a moment she allowed herself the luxury of leaning against his broad chest. Then he was putting her down on to the settee and she forced herself to move away from him.

He sat down next to her and put a gentle hand on her forehead. 'You don't feel as if you have a temperature,' he murmured, his eyes raking over her pale features in concern. 'How long have you been feeling sick?'

She shook her head. 'There's nothing wrong with me, Brant, I just need to take things easy for a while.'

'Of course there's something wrong with you.' His voice was hoarse and strained. 'You were violently sick on Friday morning and you nearly passed out on me just now.' He got to his feet and moved towards the phone.

'What are you doing?' As she struggled to sit up a golden swath of hair fell over her cheek and seemed to highlight her pale complexion, giving her an almost ethereal beauty.

'I'm ringing my doctor,' Brant told her crisply.

'But I don't need a doctor,' she protested in alarm. 'It's nothing.'

'We'll let the doctor be the judge of that.' Brant's eyebrows were drawn together in a firm uncompromising line as he started to dial.

'Please, Brant,' she pleaded, but still he paid no attention. 'There is nothing wrong with me, Brant,' she persisted and then, as he still showed no signs of putting the phone down, she said the words that had been burning inside her. 'I'm pregnant, ten weeks pregnant.'

Her words dropped into a deep chasm of silence. Brant stared at her as if she were speaking a foreign language. The phone clattered back down on to its hook. 'Ten weeks!' he repeated finally, his voice sounding as if he was in shock. 'Why didn't you tell me?'

She closed her eyes; she couldn't bear to see the recrimination on his face. 'Because you made it clear you didn't want children. I was afraid to tell you,' she murmured softly.

The silence that greeted that statement stretched out uncomfortably. 'Don't worry, Brant, I don't want anything from you. You needn't feel obligated to me,' she carried on hurriedly. 'After our divorce I'll change my name and the baby's back to McConell. I'll bring my baby up on my own.'

'The hell you will!' Brant cut in harshly. 'Don't you think I should have some say in this, considering that it is my baby as well?'

She shook her head. 'No, Brant, I don't, because I know that anything you have to say will be said out of some sense of duty or misplaced guilt. I don't want you around under those terms.' Her voice sounded rational and calm while inside she was a seething mass of mixed emotions.

'I don't want to stay around out of a sense of duty.' His voice had a husky edge to it now. 'I want to stay around because I love you.'

Her eyes flew open and stared up at him in disbelief. 'That's what I was trying to tell you in the kitchen.' He raked a hand through dark hair. 'I love you, Kelsey, and I want you as my wife. I've hated being apart from you these last few days. . .' He trailed off uncertainly. 'I've been practising that speech all the way here and it still sounds as corny as ever.'

Kelsey swallowed hard, hardly daring to believe what she was hearing. 'It sounds wonderful to me,' she whispered.

Dark eyes held green ones for a few seconds, and then

he was sitting down beside her and holding her tightly in his arms. Weakly she clung to him, unbelievable happiness flowing through her. 'I thought that you were in love with Susanna,' she murmured against his shoulder, and tears flooded into her eyes at that very thought.

'Oh, Kelsey,' he groaned, and held her a little way away from him so that he could look down into her face. 'Susanna Winters has never been anything but a mild irritation to me.'

'But you slept with her just before our wedding,' Kelsey said in a low shaking voice.

'You are joking!' Brant looked completely outraged for a moment. 'I have never slept with that woman. I've got more sense and more taste than that. She came around to my house the night before the wedding, literally threw herself at me, but I sent her packing very quickly.'

Kelsey swallowed hard. 'So you didn't go away with her at the weekend?'

'Is that what you thought?' he rasped harshly.

She nodded her head.

'There is nothing between Susanna and me and I have certainly never gone away anywhere with her.' He held Kelsey close in against him again as if frightened to let her go. 'I love you, Kelsey, more than anyone or anything in this world.'

She cuddled in against him and smiled tremulously through her tears. 'You'll have to keep telling me that, I'm having difficulty letting it sink in. I keep thinking I'm dreaming.'

Brant stroked her hair gently back from her face and kissed her tenderly. 'You first,' he whispered against her ear.

She lifted her head slightly to look up at him. 'I love you with all my heart, Brant, I always have. Even before you asked me to marry you. That was the one and only reason that I accepted your proposal.'

Brant closed his eyes as if savouring the words. 'I've been such a fool, Kelsey, such an awful fool.'

'Don't talk about the man I love like that,' Kelsey murmured with a smile.

His eyes opened and there was an answering smile in their dark depths before he said in a more serious tone, 'I've been so hung up on the past that I haven't been able to see anything clearly where you are concerned.'

'Because of Francesca?' she asked softly.

He nodded and pulled away from her slightly. 'I've never spoken to you about my marriage to Francesca. It's not something that I like talking about.'

'You don't have to tell me about it, Brant, not if it's painful for you,' she told him quickly.

'It is painful, but not for the reasons that you might think.' He wasn't looking at her, and she knew his thoughts were moving back into the past.

'I met Francesca at a party. She was the centre of attention, the most beautiful woman in the room.' He gave a bleak smile. 'And she knew it. Franky loved to play to an adoring audience.'

Kelsey could picture her: a slim, willowy, blonde beauty whom Brant had fallen for at first sight. She swallowed hard, not knowing if she really wanted to hear any more.

'She did part-time modelling when I met her but she was very ambitious, wanted to hit the big time. She came from a very wealthy background and she was used to getting what she wanted. This made her supremely confident and she pursued her career with a single-minded determination that could be quite daunting at times.' He paused, and for a moment there was silence. His thoughts were far away and Kelsey wondered if he had forgotten that she was there.

'We started to date on a regular basis. We made love.' Brant shrugged. 'She was a vibrant personality, a beautiful woman. I was captivated by her. I asked her to marry me only weeks after I had met her and she accepted.' He turned, caught the wistful look on Kelsey's face and gave a sad smile. 'Don't look like that, Kelsey, this is not the story of the perfect whirlwind romance,' he assured her drily.

'I suppose you could say that the first six months of our marriage were happy. We didn't see a lot of each other. I was heavily involved in my work, Francesca was pursuing her career, everything seemed fine. Then Francesca discovered that she was pregnant.'

Kelsey's eyes widened and her breath caught in her throat at the grimness of his tone.

'I was pleased,' Brant continued in a flat unemotional voice. 'Francesca was anything but pleased. She had just been offered a big modelling contract; it was the start of the big time for her. A baby, she said, would ruin everything. She would be tied to the house, it would spoil her figure. I tried to tell her that it didn't have to be like that. She would get her figure back, I'd cut down on my workload and we would hire a nanny so that she could go back to work. I thought that she was in agreement with that, but apparently not. She went and had an abortion without even telling me what she was doing.' His voice was filled with tension and his hands opened and closed in a kind of helpless anger.

Kelsey placed her hand over his and held it in silent sympathy, her heart going out to him. What he was telling her shocked her deeply. She had always believed implicitly that Brant's first marriage had been idyllic.

'We had the most terrible, bitter row. She broke down in tears and begged me to forgive her and understand. I tried. . . I really did try.' He raked a hand through his hair. 'We moved house. I tried to tell myself that it was Francesca's right to make her own decision over the baby, but I just couldn't come to terms with that. Then I discovered that she was lying to me about little things like whom she was having lunch with, why she was so late home some evenings. It didn't take long to find out that she had been having a long string of affairs, all calculated to help her career. A top photographer, an editor of a glossy magazine who made her his cover girl. When I confronted her with it, she just shrugged her shoulders and said the affairs didn't mean anything, they were just a means to an end.'

'Oh, Brant, I'm sorry,' Kelsey murmured, her tender heart filled with sadness.

Brant shook his head grimly. 'No, Kelsey, I'm the one who's sorry. I've allowed what's happened in the past to come between us. After my sham of a marriage I vowed that I would never get involved again. That was an easy promise to keep until I met you. From the first moment that we met I was deeply attracted to you, and that perturbed me.' He gave her a sheepish grin. 'Well, if I'm going to be truthful I may as well tell you that it scared the hell out of me!'

Her eyebrows rose at that but she said nothing; she was too busy hanging on his every word.

'You came from a similar background to Francesca's. I watched as you went after promotion within the company and I told myself that you were as spoilt and as coldly calculating as she was. Yet everything you said and did contradicted me on that and I found it harder and harder to stay away. It was pure torture watching you go out with Daniel. Jealousy started to creep in on me and I realised that I wanted you like crazy.'

Kelsey shook her head in wonderment. 'I never realised. You never showed any sign of being interested in me.'

'I knew that if I did, if I took you in my arms, there would be no going back.' He smiled down at her and there was a brief teasing light in his eyes. 'You have the words "Serious Stuff" written all over you, do you know that?'

She grinned. 'I'm very glad to hear that. We'll just keep them there, shall we?'

'For ever and a day.' He nodded, and then continued more seriously. 'So you see, when Joe died I thought over the terms of his will and it seemed to me to be my ideal opportunity. I could have you in my life, I could make love to you and I didn't have to risk getting emotionally involved.' He gave a self-derisive laugh. 'I reckoned without you, Kelsey. Once I had experienced your sweetness, your warmth, I was lost. The first time that I made love to you it hit me with forceful intensity that I was totally and irrevocably in love with you. From then on all the rules that I had made about keeping myself emotionally apart from you just started to backfire on me. I wanted to tell you how I felt but I just couldn't find the words. Then I started to imagine that you were really in love with Daniel and I felt too much of a fool to say them.'

She shook her head. 'There is no room in my heart for anyone else but you, Brant.' She gave him a sudden teasing grin. 'And our baby, of course.'

He smiled and one hand trailed in a tender caress down the side of her face. 'What I said about not having children. . .' He shook his head. 'I don't know what on earth made me say it, except that I thought that it would be something you would want to hear. I thought that your career——'

She placed a gentle hand over his mouth. 'My career *is* important to me, Brant,' she told him gently. 'But I'm not Francesca. I'm going to juggle babies and career with a dexterity that will astound you.'

He laughed at that. 'You never fail to astound me, Kelsey; you do it every day.'

For a while there was no more talking as his lips found hers and they lost themselves in the sweetness of love.

'By the way,' he murmured finally as he lifted his head, 'you *are* going to come back home with me, aren't you?' There was the tiniest note of uncertainty in his voice.

'I don't know.' She sat back from him and pretended to give the matter some thought. 'We will have to make a whole new set of rules.'

'Oh?' For a moment he looked genuinely perplexed.

'Yes.' She nodded her head seriously. 'I'm going to make some conditions of my own now and you've got to stick to them. First. . .' she started to count them out on her fingers '. . .you've got to tell me that you love me at least once a day——'

She never did get to finish, because suddenly he was reaching for her with a low growl of happiness. 'I think I can manage that,' he told her with absolute confidence.

HARLEQUIN

Romance®

and WEDDINGS go together—
especially in June!
So don't miss next month's title in

THE BRIDAL COLLECTION

LOVE YOUR ENEMY
by Ellen James

THE BRIDE led the anti-Jarrett forces.
THE GROOM was Jarrett!
THE WEDDING? An Attraction of Opposites!

Available this month in
THE BRIDAL COLLECTION

THE MAN YOU'LL MARRY
by Debbie Macomber
Harlequin Romance (#3196)
Wherever Harlequin books are sold.

OVER THE YEARS, TELEVISION HAS BROUGHT
THE LIVES AND LOVES OF MANY CHARACTERS INTO
YOUR HOMES. NOW HARLEQUIN INTRODUCES YOU
TO THE TOWN AND PEOPLE OF

One small town—twelve terrific love stories.

GREAT READING... GREAT SAVINGS... AND A FABULOUS
FREE GIFT!

Each book set in Tyler is a self-contained love story; together, the
twelve novels stitch the fabric of the community.

By collecting proofs-of-purchase found in each Tyler book, you can
receive a fabulous gift, ABSOLUTELY FREE! And use our special
Tyler coupons to save on your next TYLER book purchase.

Join us for the fourth TYLER book,
MONKEY WRENCH by Nancy Martin.

*Can elderly Rose Atkins successfully bring a new love into
granddaughter Susannah's life?*

BIG SUMMER READ

Summer Reading At Its Best

In July, Harlequin and Silhouette bring readers the Big Summer Read Program. Heat up your summer with these four exciting new novels by top Harlequin and Silhouette authors.

SOMEWHERE IN TIME by Barbara Bretton
YESTERDAY COMES TOMORROW by Rebecca Flanders
A DAY IN APRIL by Mary Lynn Baxter
LOVE CHILD by Patricia Coughlin

From time travel to fame and fortune, this program offers something for everyone.

Available at your favorite retail outlet.

BSR

Harlequin

JANELLE TAYLOR

Valley of Fire

HARLEQUIN IS PROUD TO PRESENT *VALLEY OF FIRE* BY JANELLE TAYLOR—AUTHOR OF TWENTY-TWO BOOKS, INCLUDING SIX *NEW YORK TIMES* BESTSELLERS

VALLEY OF FIRE—the warm and passionate story of Kathy Alexander, a famous romance author, and Steven Winngate, entrepreneur and owner of the magazine that intended to expose the real Kathy ''Brandy'' Alexander to her fans.

Don't miss VALLEY OF FIRE, available in May.